THE SINS OF THE ORC

AN MM MONSTER ROMANCE

FINLEY FENN

Editing: Eris Adderly
Cover art: Qaisan
Cover design: Sylvia at The Book Brander

This is a work of fiction. Names, characters, places, and incidents are the product of the author's imagination or are used fictitiously. Any resemblance to actual persons living or dead, business establishments, events, or locales is entirely coincidental.

The Sins of the Orc

ALSO BY FINLEY FENN

Sign up at www.finleyfenn.com for bonus stories and epilogues, delicious orc artwork, complete content guidance, news about upcoming books, and more!

ABOUT THE SINS OF THE ORC

He's fallen too far to save... but his enemy is going to try.

In a world of warring orcs and men, Kesst of Clan Ash-Kai is a pawn. A pretty, pliant plaything, bound to the cruelest orcs in the realm.

Until the new healer storms in.

He's huge, hostile, and hideous, with a powerful scarred body and terrifying ancient magic. And it only takes one disastrous meeting before he and Kesst are bitter enemies, and Kesst vows to see the vile brute destroyed...

And then **a sudden, deadly attack** hurls his helpless body straight at the healer's feet.

Kesst fully expects to be mocked, belittled, abandoned to his doom— **but instead, his new enemy picks him up.**

Soothes his wounds.

And carries him home...

Soon Kesst is trapped in a tiny sickroom beneath Orc Mountain, caught in the thrall of the healer's impossible magic. In the surprising gentleness of his touch. In the strength of his stubborn, seductive safety...

But with his horrid handlers close on their scent, Kesst can't possibly be falling for his forbidden foe... can he? **Can a healer save him from his sins... or destroy him?**

AUTHOR'S NOTE

Dear reader,

Thank you so much for joining me for this MM orc tale!

If you're new to my orcs (welcome!!!), this book reads entirely as a stand-alone. However, if you're familiar with my ongoing Orc Sworn series, this book goes back in time, and takes place several years before the events of *The Lady and the Orc*.

Kesst's story is about healing, recovery, and finding love and peace amidst the darkness. However, it therefore does include some dark themes, emotions, and power dynamics, and Kesst's initial situation may be difficult for some readers. If you'd like full details on what to expect, please visit this book's page on my website at www.finleyfenn.com.

Finally, I know the word "sins" is a loaded term for a lot of us, but please be reassured that it's not at all used to devalue anyone's orientation in this book.

Thank you again for reading!

With warmest appreciation,
    Finley

To the ever-fabulous MK
(a.k.a. Kesst's bestie!)

1

The new healer, Kesst decided, was an arse. A stodgy, stuffy, stick-up-the-rump *arse*.

"You shouldn't file your claws like that," the arse was currently saying, his voice hard, his eyes glowering down at Kesst's perfectly manicured hand. "Of course they're going to get infected. Can't you see how that's irritating your clawbed?"

Kesst frowned straight back at the stuffy new healer— Efterar, his name apparently was, and he was supposedly from Clan Ash-Kai, too. Though he'd only shown up at Orc Mountain a moon or two ago, and gods only knew where he'd crawled out from. The southern clans, most likely, given his square blockish build, his scarred, craggy face, and his utter dearth of manners, or attractiveness, or taste.

"My claws look better this way," Kesst countered, flipping his long black hair over his shoulder. "More refined. Less... orc-like."

The healer's disapproving eyes snapped up to Kesst's face, fully meeting his gaze for the first time in this highly unpleasant little contretemps. "You *are* an orc, Ash-Kai," he growled, crossing his big arms against his grey tunic. "What, do you want to look *human*?"

Despite himself, Kesst twitched a step back toward the camp tunnel's grimy wall behind him, while an odd, curious chill flickered up his spine. *Magic.* This stuffy grump healer had the old Ash-Kai magic, of course he did—and of course Kesst would be able to taste it. Like knowing like, and all that rubbish.

But gods, it was strong. Stronger than it had any right to be, on such an ugly odious curmudgeon. A curmudgeon who was *still* glaring at Kesst, as though instead of getting bored and fretful on a raid—and taking out his anxiety on his claws— Kesst had just gone and shat on this bastard's clean, irritatingly large black boots.

"Well, maybe I *do* want to look human," Kesst belatedly replied, giving his coolest, blandest smile. "Maybe I'd rather not be sent off into this godsforsaken raid tomorrow to have my entrails carved out by desperate humans, hmmm?"

The healer's head tilted, his eyes narrowed to thin, skeptical slits. "They wouldn't send *you* out to fight," he said, with a cursory, dismissive glance up and down Kesst's slim, bare-chested form. "That's ridiculous."

It took a considerable effort for Kesst to hold the smile to his face, though his gaze had reflexively dropped, down to his reddened, painful finger. "Indeed," he said tightly. "But alas, worse things have happened."

The silence felt thick, suddenly, curdling with an unfamiliar scent—and Kesst realized it was from the healer. His scent had simmered low and unobtrusive until now, sweet but thankfully not too strong—but now it had a sharp, bitter edge on it, almost like anger.

"What do you mean, worse things have happened?" the healer demanded, his voice just as sharp as his scent. "To *you*?"

The smile had fully slipped from Kesst's mouth now, his

eyes still intent on his infected finger. And if he had been a loyal brother, a brave and powerful Ash-Kai, he would have laughed, and waved the question away. He'd have said, with convincing confidence, that he would never be sent out to fight as punishment. Or left outside alone in the freezing cold for days on end. Or loaned out to the best fighters after a battle, while the rest of his clan watched, and envied, and *approved*.

"Look, you can't really think you've walked into some absurd orc utopia here, right?" Kesst finally said, his voice not nearly as light as he'd meant, as he gave a jerky wave at the horrid cramped tunnel around them, the distinct scents of blood and hunger just beyond. "I don't know where you've been hiding away all this time, healer, but we're at *war*. The humans want to *destroy* us. We never have enough food, or gold, or fighters, or sons. It's *rubbish*, this life, and we're trapped in it to the death. And if you had any sense whatsoever"—he dragged in breath, met the healer's eyes—"you would fuck off, back to wherever the hell you came from, *forever*!"

It came out far too loud, ringing against the tunnel's too-close walls, and for the briefest of instants, something stuttered in the healer's scent. Something dark and sour, nearly strong enough to choke Kesst's already-constricted throat.

"Right," the healer finally said, his voice flat and emotionless again, his eyes carefully blank—and then his big hand swiftly reached out, brushed against Kesst's finger, and dropped again. "Do you need anything else dealt with, then?"

Kesst blinked at the healer, at that emptiness in his eyes—and then down at his own oddly tingling finger. At how the previously reddened, inflamed skin had somehow faded back to its usual grey, his black, filed-off claw looking unnervingly fragile against it.

"Oh," Kesst said thinly, as he kept blinking toward it. "No. Nothing else. Nothing the likes of *you* could fix, at least."

He'd attempted a dismissive sneer toward the healer,

though perhaps it came out more like a grimace—but the healer had flinched backwards, all the same. And then his big body abruptly whirled around, swinging out a long black braid behind him, as his hand snatched for a full waterskin he'd had propped against a rock. And then he dumped out the waterskin over his hands, and began frantically rubbing them together.

Oh. The healer was... washing himself. As if... as if he'd desperately needed to scrub off the taint of Kesst's scent, when they'd scarcely even *touched*.

And gods, it should not have hurt like that. Kesst should not have given one flying fuck about this stuffy ugly healer from the backwoods, with his stupid judgement, and his stupid naivety, and his stupid damned magic. Magic Kesst could still feel *inside* him, in his own damned finger, still tingling with bizarre, alarming strength. And with a low, astonishing sweetness...

"And next time, maybe warn me before you start fucking with my insides," Kesst snapped at the healer's back, because he needed to say something, *anything*, to shove this feeling away. "And just so you know, I happen to have some *very* powerful friends around here, hmmm? So if you'd actually like to survive this delightful new job of yours, you *may* want to take better care in how you treat me!"

And was Kesst happy to see the way the healer's broad shoulders hunched, he was, he *was*. "You came to be healed, so I did my job, and healed you," the healer hissed, without looking, as he poured out more water over his hands. "So fuck you."

Kesst instinctively recoiled, his body stiffening, his own hands balling into fists. "You only *wish*," he snarled back at the healer, brittle and scathing. "From the smell of you, you've never fucked once in your sheltered little *life*."

It had only been a suspicion, though one that had kept growing as Kesst had kept standing here, feeling the healer's magic *inside* him, while still breathing in that sweet, subtle, unnervingly appealing scent. And maybe that was why he was reacting like this, why this heinous stuffy arsehole was setting him off like this, like—

"And from the smell of *you*, you've had half the orcs in that damned *mountain* fucking with your insides," the healer growled back. "You think that's *better*?!"

He'd whirled around to glare at Kesst, his big wet hand waving furiously at Kesst's weak, skinny form, his tainted, used, broken scent. The sharp movement even spraying droplets of water on Kesst's chest, his face, as if in some pathetic attempt to clean him, when they both knew he'd never be clean again, ever.

"You prudish, presumptuous *prick*," Kesst gulped, as he reflexively scrubbed at the water, brushing it away, away. "How *dare* you. I'll have you know, I—I—"

He what? Damn it, *what*? He was known for his wit, his smart mouth, his uncanny ability to sway his superiors with his grace and beauty and charm. For being the sweet, pretty, eloquent human most of them would never have, down to the weakness of his body, and the blunted tips of his claws.

But he was still just standing here, staring at this horrid healer's face, and realizing, with a jolt of shock, that he was very near to weeping. Weeping over this stodgy, stuffy, stick-up-the-rump *arse*, for reasons he couldn't bear to examine too closely.

"Look, I—I'm sorry," the healer cut in, his eyes and his scent flaring, his hand darting toward Kesst, and away again. "I shouldn't have said that. Don't cry. Please."

Kesst flinched, not only at those words—that open admission of his blatant weakness—but at that look in the healer's eyes. The... *pity*. Now this belligerent bastard was pitying him, because he was standing here in a filthy camp tunnel and weeping, like the utter failure of an orc he was.

"I am *not crying*," Kesst finally managed, even as he frantically blinked back the cursed wetness behind his eyes. "And I have no need whatsoever for your apologies, or your pity, or your horribly invasive 'healing'. And I will thank the gods if I never have to set eyes on your hideous face ever *again*, let alone taste your vile magic *inside* me!"

And again, he was glad to see the way the healer twitched, the way his big shoulders hunched higher. The way his mouth snapped open, as if he were about to retaliate—but then he winced, and squeezed his eyes shut. While that dark bitterness again twisted into his magic, souring the air between them, strong enough that Kesst nearly retched.

"Right," the healer finally replied, his low voice so wooden, so empty. "Right. I'll note that."

And that was it, surely. Kesst was surely the victor in this hellish little encounter, whatever the hell it had been. So why the hell was he still weeping, why was there the overpowering urge to shout, to step closer, to *apologize*—

"Good," he spat toward the healer, before it was too late, too late. "You do that."

And without waiting for an answer, he whirled around, and fled into the darkness.

2

———

The next time he set eyes upon the new healer, Kesst was being railed in the rump by the most loathsome orc in the entire realm.

Or perhaps second most loathsome, Kesst mentally amended, as he darted a glance across the fire, toward the crouching form of Orc Mountain's huge, repulsive captain—Kaugir, of Clan Ash-Kai. Who was blatantly looking back toward Kesst, his beady eyes gleaming, his long tongue deliberately licking the fat and blood off his thick clawed fingers.

"Ach, that is the way, Skald," Kaugir grunted, his leering gaze flicking up to the orc behind Kesst, who was still pounding away with tedious enthusiasm. "Make him forget all about Ofnir, ach?"

The bastard. Kesst felt himself betray a full-body flinch, enough that Skald behind him—inside him—barked a loud, grating laugh, and sharply swatted his arse. "You'll not be getting off to memories of Ofnir whilst I plough you, wench."

Kesst belatedly moaned and shook his head, tossing his hair up, arching his back. "Who's Ofnir?" he breathed, with creditable nonchalance. "Can't remember."

Skald barked another approving laugh, and across the fire even Kaugir looked grimly amused. And Kesst actually managed a smile toward Kaugir, a flirtatious flutter of his eyelashes, knowing—thanks to some lucky quirk of the gods— that the cruel, deadly captain of Orc Mountain could only ever get hard for human women, and for the prospect of siring his sons upon them. And therefore, Kaugir had always been happy to leave Kesst to the rest of his hangers-on instead—and most of all to his two hulking, powerful Hands. Skald, of Clan Ash-Kai, and Ofnir, of Clan Skai.

And though Ofnir had been blessedly dead for several moons now, Kesst could still feel the agonizing drag of his vicious claws, could still taste the sickly sweetness of his distinctive Skai scent. So strong that it still overpowered every other orc's scent upon him, Skald's included—though at this rate, Skald was giving Ofnir a good run for that highly dubious prize.

"You like that, pretty wench?" Skald grunted at Kesst, from where he'd picked up speed behind him. "You should love to have only *my* ploughing for all the rest of your days, ach?"

Kesst moaned some semblance of breathless agreement, even as he inwardly cursed Skald, and his own rotten existence. Skald wasn't quite as vile as Ofnir had been, but after Kaugir, he was most certainly the last orc Kesst would have chosen to make some kind of actual claim upon him next. Skald was loud, rude, arrogant, aggressive, with no gentleness or subtlety whatsoever—and he took inordinate pride in his fat, admittedly impressive prick, and in how it invariably left his conquests limping and wincing for days on end.

And while Kesst couldn't deny enjoying an oversized prick—as well as a good proper pounding now and then—it was just like Skald to so carelessly wield it like this, right before a gruelling two-day trek back to Orc Mountain, during which Kesst would inevitably be loaded down with goods they'd acquired from today's raid. Gods, he hated travelling, he hated kneeling in the dirt, he hated this stupid endless war, he hated his entire damned *life*—

And it was then, as Kesst was groaning, keening into Skald's onslaught, that he met the new healer's eyes. The healer had been walking past the fire, with a hunk of fresh meat clutched in his big hand—a cut from the day's kill, a felled deer at the edge of the clearing—but now he'd frozen in place behind Kaugir, and was staring. Staring straight at Kesst, bared on his hands and knees in the filth and ash, with Skald still pounding away behind him.

Something hot and shameful abruptly curdled in Kesst's belly, and he could feel his face and ears flushing scarlet, in a way that had nothing to do with Skald or the fire. This stodgy, stuffy healer was staring at him, he was judging him, and he was... *pitying* him. As if Kesst were a weak, contemptible disappointment, rather than a clever, pragmatic orc who knew exactly what he was doing. Ingratiating himself with the most powerful orcs in the realm, and revelling in this one's massive prick, like the beautiful, eager size queen he was.

"Oh, that's good," Kesst breathed, again fluttering his lashes and tossing his hair over his shoulder. "So nice and thick. *Love* feeling it inside me."

Skald barked another approving laugh, gave him another swat. And Kesst managed to purr another heated, convincing moan, his eyes again fixed on the healer. On how the healer still hadn't moved, and how the hunk of rib he was holding had suddenly bent at an unnatural angle. As if—as if his hand had somehow snapped the bone inside it.

"Ach, I ken that new healer likes seeing you get your due, wench," crooned Skald behind Kesst. "Or mayhap he is jealous. Wishes he could have a turn."

But Kesst already knew better, because that look in the healer's frozen eyes certainly wasn't jealousy, or envy, or approval. No, no, it was still that same damned *pity*, scraping up Kesst's arched spine, clawing at him, choking in his throat...

And Kesst couldn't bear it, it was worse than Skald, worse than the dirt and ash beneath him, worse than Kaugir's thick greasy fingers. And he had to fight against it, had to drag for his dignity, his pride, *something*...

"Oh, he only *wishes*," Kesst heard himself say, far too loudly, flashing his coldest smile toward the still-staring healer. "Didn't you know, Skald dearest, our newest, ugliest arrival has never been touched *once* in his smug, sheltered little life?"

And oh, there it was again, the satisfying recoil of the healer's body, the flare of hurt across his ugly face. And the way Skald and Kaugir both laughed, Kaugir now turning and eyeing the healer with a contemptuous, calculating interest that certainly hadn't been there before.

"Ach, another bewitcher," Kaugir said, his lip curling. "Who costs us much good food and coin, and gives us only magic tricks in return. My stubborn, soft-hearted son claims this new one cannot even fight, either."

Kesst could see the healer's big body stiffening even more, and behind him Skald loudly scoffed. "So the bewitcher does not fight, and he does not fuck," he said. "What good is he to us, then?"

It was the perfect opening, the perfect opportunity for Kesst to point out that this bewitcher was indeed no good whatsoever, based on his own abysmal experience the day before—but suddenly, he couldn't seem to make himself speak. And instead, it took considerable effort to even muster a laugh, to keep the smile painfully pasted on his face, while the healer just kept staring at him with those wide, wounded eyes.

And gods, it was ridiculous, because Kesst should be truly enjoying this moment, shouldn't he? He was just giving that smug bastard exactly what he'd asked for, what he damn well deserved. So why did it keep feeling so wrong, why was there something so much like bile, rising up in his throat?

"Ach, you shall thus keep your eye on that bewitcher, Skald," Kaugir was saying now, as he spat out a bone into the fire. "If he does not soon learn to make himself useful, mayhap you shall teach him some true orc ways. That ought to be a joy to witness, ach?"

And when Skald laughed, laughed like it was the most amusing thing he'd ever heard in his life, Kesst somehow laughed again, too. Grinding his victory harder, deeper, colder, watching it catch and wrench in the healer's too-expressive eyes. Until the healer finally turned and lurched away, his eyes squeezing shut, his hand clamped over his mouth. Almost as though he felt sick, too.

"Or cull him," Kaugir continued, with gut-churning casualness. "We are at war. We have no spare food and coin to waste on idlers, ach?"

Kesst's body betrayed an unmistakable flinch, but he was fine, fine, better than ever. Of course he was. And when the healer disappeared into the darkness, hopefully never to be seen again, Kesst most certainly didn't notice, or care. And instead, he tossed his head, arched his back, and howled his victory to the sky.

P redictably, the next morning found Kesst trudging bow-legged through the forest, and awkwardly rolling a huge, heavy barrel before him.

"Are you well, brother?" asked a familiar deep voice, and Kesst rolled his eyes as he glanced sideways toward his Ash-Kai brother Grimarr. Who currently had a barrel perched on one big shoulder, and a gigantic sack slung over the other—and who, despite all this, hadn't even appeared to break a sweat, the infuriating lout.

"Perfectly fine," Kesst replied, his voice thin, his gaze darting back toward the rest of the distant band ahead. "I *love* travelling. *Such* a delight, as always."

Grimarr loudly snorted, and shifted the barrel on his shoulder. "I could likely handle this," he said, nodding at Kesst's barrel, "if you could help me tie this sack on my back."

Now it was Kesst's turn to snort, his head shaking. "I appreciate your gallantry, Grim," he replied, "but you know how your father and Skald like to see me earning my keep."

The words came out sharper than Kesst meant, his eyes

again angling up toward where he could just make out Kaugir and Skald, at the front of the band ahead. Surrounded by their ever-present entourage of elite Skai and Ash-Kai hangers-on, all of them carrying nothing, as usual—while behind them, every other orc in the party was loaded down with sacks and barrels. Even the wounded ones, and even—Kesst frowned at the sight—that damned healer, trailing along at the rear of the band, carrying a heavy-looking pack on his broad shoulders. Making himself somewhat useful, at least, and Kesst felt his stomach twist as he watched, while Kaugir's words from the night before echoed through his skull.

Keep your eye on that one, Skald. Teach him some true orc ways. Or cull him.

Beside Kesst, Grimarr had given a low, disapproving growl, in an unnerving echo of Kesst's own deepest thoughts—and when he glanced sideways, Grimarr was frowning up at the band, too. His eyes gone dark and angry on Kaugir's distant form, his teeth visibly bared. Showing his very clear disapproval, in a way that no other orc would have ever dared to do.

And while Kesst would never risk speaking it aloud, he was desperately, absurdly grateful for that constant simmering antagonism between Grimarr and his ghastly father. After Ofnir's death, Kesst had fully expected Grimarr to finally step up, and take his proper place as Kaugir's obvious successor and protege—but instead, Grimarr had only seemed to ease further away. Always bringing up the rear of the bands like this, and going off on his own mysterious missions, and dragging back random new orcs like the healer. And lately, Grimarr had even taken two orcs—Baldr, a new arrival from the Grisk clan, and Drafli, yet another horrid Skai like Ofnir—and had rather begun treating them as though they were his own two Hands. Almost the way Kaugir had done with Skald and Ofnir.

"Plotting something, brother?" Kesst asked pleasantly, with

his blandest smile. "I couldn't help but notice that your two obedient shadows have disappeared, again?"

Grimarr shot Kesst his familiar reproachful look, his jaw tightening in his scarred cheek. "Baldr and Drafli are only scouting ahead," he said flatly. "The scents of armed men are strong upon this route, ach?"

Right. That was something Kesst had heard Grimarr quietly raising with his father, before they'd broken camp that morning—but as usual, Kaugir had scoffed at his son's concerns, and blithely continued on, just as he'd planned. Just like the short-sighted, self-absorbed bastard he'd always been.

"Are you sure you will not let me take that?" Grimarr asked now, again nodding toward Kesst's barrel, and slowing his long strides. "Or mayhap"—his too-aware eyes flicked down to Kesst's ridiculous gait—"call Efterar back here to heal you?"

The growl burned from Kesst's throat before he could catch it, his head whipping back and forth. "I do *not* need healing, most of all from that smug bastard," he retorted. "He is *such* a stuffy stodgy arse, you must know. Where did you even find him, anyway?"

Grimarr's glance at Kesst was surprised, his thick brows raised. "Ach, is aught amiss with him?" he asked. "Have you not yet seen his work? He shall be a great, great gift to us all, I ken."

Kesst couldn't help noticing that Grimarr hadn't actually answered the part about where the healer had come from—and also, that there was now suspicion darkening his too-perceptive eyes. "Efterar has not already run afoul of my father, has he?" he added, quieter. "Have you heard aught, upon this?"

Kesst's cursed throat reflexively swallowed, and Grimarr abruptly stopped walking, shifting enough of his sack that he could reach and grip at Kesst's arm. "Kesst," he hissed, even lower. "This healer may alter *all* for us. If my father turns his eye toward him, or makes *any* move against him, you will speak to me of this. You *must*."

"Yes, yes, fine," Kesst said, too quickly, his eyes angling away, his face heating. His stomach again horribly twisting, the temptation to blurt out the whole stupid story rising in his throat—but he forcibly shoved it back, and bit at his lip. Kaugir hadn't truly made a *move* toward the healer, had he? At least, not yet... right? And the healer had fully deserved it... hadn't he?

"I thank you, brother," Grimarr said, his scent swarming with almost painful intensity now, as his hand gave Kesst's arm a firm little shake. "You have a sharp eye and a quick tongue, and your help in this means much to me."

And gods, Kesst's traitorous eyes were actually prickling, and he held them purposefully away, on the thick forest beyond Grimarr's shoulder. Damn Grimarr and his damned earnestness, his ceaseless plotting, his constant quiet implication that Kesst was on his side, party to the cause. That Kesst wasn't just a pretty plaything, but a valued asset, a collaborator, an informant. A spy. Which was truly, patently ludicrous, because passing on a few bits of news and gossip here and there surely amounted to nothing in the larger scheme of things, right?

"Such untoward flattery, brother," Kesst heard himself replying, his lashes fluttering, his body leaning a little into Grimarr's touch. "If this is a backhanded attempt to get into my trousers, you know you only ever need to ask."

He'd meant it to sound light, but damn him if it didn't come out almost pleading, and surely pathetic, too. Because he'd been there with Grimarr, years before, and not only had the devious lout been a considerate lover, but an unfairly enthralling one, too. Warm, commanding, affectionate, with a big powerful body, a smooth, steady scent, and a highly impressive prick. As if it had all been perfectly calibrated to poke and peel at Kesst's cold, shrivelled heart.

You ken I shall always be fond of you, Grimarr had told Kesst when he'd ended it, after a particularly humiliating confession on Kesst's part. *But I could never take you as my mate, ach? Not amidst all this.*

This. This, with the endless war. With his foul father. With the anger and the plotting, the constant jockeying for power and women and sons. And, too, with the way Grimarr still seemed to crave women with an almost pathetic desperation, despite how disastrous his previous attempts had been.

And Kesst knew that, and why had he even said that, and fired yet more darkness into his best brother's eyes. Gods, what madness had even come over him these past days, and he inexplicably glanced up at the ever-smaller backs of the party ahead, at the distant sight of the healer's broad shoulders, bowed low under the weight of his pack.

"And you know I'm just jesting, obviously," Kesst said, with a painful-feeling attempt at a jocular smile. "Your prick doesn't even come close to Skald's. Paltry in comparison, really. Could barely even feel it."

That was surely relief in Grimarr's eyes, but with a tinge of ruefulness, too. Because they both knew how much Kesst had loved it, how he'd keened and wailed upon it, and then collapsed into Grimarr's safe warm arms. And curse him, but was he about to start weeping, *again*? What the *hell*?

"Ach, brother, I ken how it is," Grimarr said now, his head tilting, his breath exhaling—and Kesst was suddenly very aware that they weren't talking about his prick anymore. "You ken it shall not be much longer, now. With this healer now on our side, we—"

But Kesst never found out what the healer would change, because Grimarr's nostrils abruptly flared, his head whipping around—and in a strange, jolting flash, he leapt. Tossing the barrel away, lunging toward Kesst, knocking him aside, fear and fury screaming through his scent—

But it was too late, too late, because the crossbow bolt was already here. Sinking its sharpened steel deep into Kesst's chest, and shattering out pain as he screamed.

4

———

For the rest of the morning, Kesst was subjected to a highly unpleasant barrage of agony, indignity, and humiliation.

It began with Grimarr shouting at the band ahead, sending half its orcs running back at once, while he himself roughly yanked at Kesst's hands—which were already losing feeling as they clutched desperately at the steel bolt embedded beneath his collarbone—and pinned them painfully to the side. And then Grimarr alternated between hollering orders at his fighters, who were now pouring into the forest behind them, and barking at Efterar to come at once, faster, *now*.

And curse the healer but he'd instantly obeyed, he'd rushed back toward them, he was here, looming over Kesst's shuddering, whimpering body. His ugly face gone stark and pale, his eyes wide, his mouth contorting. While his big hand hovered over the bolt in Kesst's upper chest, close enough that fresh red blood spurted onto his palm—but wait, the healer was shaking his head, he was saying no, no, *no*?!

"I shouldn't touch him," he breathed at Grimarr, as his

mouth clamped into a tight grimace. "He said he couldn't bear any more of my magic inside him, he—"

"DO IT!" Grimarr roared, straight into the healer's face, before glancing over his shoulder, and ducking as another bolt soared through the air, just over their heads. "*Now!*"

And with that, he stood up and kicked off, screaming as he yanked his scimitar from his belt. Leaving Kesst lying there behind him, bleeding out onto the earth, with this damned healer kneeling over him, and looking so pained that Kesst might have thought *he* was the one with the bolt buried beneath his skin.

"Sorry about this," the healer said, his mouth still grimacing, his hand settling wide and gentle against Kesst's shoulder—and then his other hand grasped the bolt, and yanked. While more raw, screaming agony tore through Kesst's destroyed chest, his entire body reflexively writhing, his mouth choking broken at the sky.

But the healer was hurling the bolt away—at least it hadn't been barbed—and now both his hands were pressed flat to Kesst's chest, his eyes closed. And Kesst could feel that sweet, sweet magic pouring into him, flooding him full and deep. Not erasing the pain, no—but the blood had already stopped spurting, and Kesst now felt that telltale prickle inside him, seeking, finding, knowing.

"*Need to move,*" barked Abjorn in Aelakesh as he raced back toward them again. "*Back to mountain. I can carry Kesst?*"

For an instant, the healer's magic inside Kesst stuttered, his brow creasing as he glanced up at Abjorn's frowning, expectant face. And Kesst's distant thoughts were lurching again, realizing something, something new. The healer didn't speak his own people's language. How in the gods' names had that happened? Hadn't he grown up among the southern clans? Had he not spent time with any orcs at *all*?

"Need to move," Kesst gasped at the healer, his voice

someone else's—but the very fact that he could still breathe and speak meant that maybe his lungs had been spared, maybe. "Abjorn can carry me."

But that was another hitch in the healer's magic, suddenly, something that might have been fear. "No," he snapped back, his eyes again intent on Kesst's wound, as the feel of the magic working inside him changed, almost as if focusing on something else. "He'll kill you. I'll do it."

He'd do it. And wait, Abjorn would *kill* him? Gods, was Kesst dying? He hadn't even made it to thirty damned summers, and now he was *dying*?!

And oh, surely he was, with the way the agony jolted and wailed as the healer's strong arms slid beneath his knees and his shoulders, and hoisted him bodily up against his broad chest. The movement undoubtedly careful, but still so horrifying that Kesst's writhing body retched, and nearly vomited up onto the healer's tunic.

But somehow—*impossibly*—he could feel the healer's magic swiftly flipping to his stomach, his throat, that touch briefly soothing it, calming it, before flicking back to his wounded chest. All this, despite the way his arms were still tightly trapped beneath Kesst's body, and his gaze was now straight ahead, his legs taking slow, deliberate steps.

And even through the agony, Kesst found himself distantly wondering at how the hell the healer could possibly be doing all this. How anyone's magic could possibly be strong enough to manage this. Carrying him, and assessing how he felt, and instantly addressing it, fixing it—and wait, now Kesst could feel that magic briefly flicking to his head, while the ongoing screeching pain abruptly faded. Sinking off and away into the distance, until it was almost negligible. And in response, Kesst felt his body suddenly relaxing into the healer's capable arms, his relieved breath exhaling in a sound much like a sob.

This was... impossible. This wasn't just magic. This was a... a gift. *A great, great gift*, Grimarr had said.

"Am I going to die?" Kesst heard himself croak, because despite the healer's clearly spectacular competence, that fear was still shouting, still here. So powerful he might have retched again, if not for yet another soft brush of the healer's magic against his churning stomach.

"No, you're not dying," the healer replied, his voice firm, his gaze still straight ahead. "Not if I can help it."

Oh. And he sounded so... certain. So stubborn. And blinking up at the healer's set face, his taut jaw, while that magic kept furiously working inside him, Kesst felt himself relaxing even deeper, sinking into the strength of those strong arms. Into this... safety.

And somehow, in that moment, everything else seemed to wash away, too. Not only the pain, but the shock, the fear, the distant sounds of battle, the barked voices and orders. And instead there was just this, this healer's warm steady body against him, this unthinkable magic inside him, that grim determination all over his hard, scarred face.

And as Kesst kept blinking up at the healer's face, it vaguely occurred to his stuttering brain that it really wasn't as hideous as he'd first supposed. He'd perhaps made that fundamental miscalculation, the one that was all too easy to do with their kind, confusing scars and wounds with ugliness. Because beneath all those scars, the healer's face was still strong. Symmetrical. His jaw square, his grey skin smooth, his pointed ears long and well-shaped, his mouth wry and expressive. And those were surely even smile-lines, gathered at the corners of his dark, frowning eyes.

And perhaps it was those lines, suggesting that this orc had, at least at some point in his life, known happiness. Or perhaps it was the way the magic was still working, still twining so deep and powerful inside Kesst's wounded chest. Or perhaps the way the pain and shock still felt impossibly, unthinkably distant, his thoughts now swirling with an odd light giddiness that didn't feel natural at all...

But whatever it was, Kesst's cursed mouth had opened, asking the inexplicably crucial question that had somehow overtaken all the rest. "If you're this good," his slurred voice said, "why'd you never fix your face?"

The healer's big body stiffened, his magic inside Kesst briefly stuttering—and gods, how half-witted *was* Kesst, truly, to be insulting the orc who was currently carrying him, easing his pain, and saving his life? The orc who could so easily toss him aside, forever, and keep on walking?

But the healer didn't toss him. Didn't even condemn him. And instead, Kesst could feel his impossible magic refocusing, still healing him, helping him, despite his cursed mouth. Despite everything Kesst had said and done the night before. *Teach him some true orc ways, or cull him...*

"I've always had more important things to deal with," the healer finally replied. "My face isn't a priority."

Kesst's mouth somehow scoffed before he could stop it, twitching a distant flare of pain through his chest. "Looking good," his thin voice informed the healer, "is *always* a priority."

The healer's magic didn't falter this time, just kept on working—now touching at where that pain had flared—though that was surely more tightness on his already-tight mouth. "No, it isn't," he replied. "I don't care what other people think of me."

It took Kesst a moment to digest that, to recover from the almost breathtaking ease—and the sheer appalling recklessness—in those words. The healer didn't care what other people thought of him. He didn't *care*?! Gods, what was that like? How would that feel? And had he not heard what Kaugir and Skald had said about him the night before? How they wanted to teach him? *Cull* him?

"You should care," Kesst croaked, with a bitter, guilty-feeling grimace. "There are... eyes on you. *Watching* you."

And gods, the more his swirling brain thought about it, the more that guilt just kept growing, crunching in his belly, flaring more pain up into his chest. Yes, the healer had been a stuffy judgemental arse, but he surely hadn't deserved Kesst sending Skald and Kaugir after him for that. And despite having been there, having witnessed Kesst's retaliation firsthand, the healer was *still* treating him like this? Still showing him such astonishing kindness, like it didn't even matter?

"And how my face looks is going to help that?" the healer replied now, his bottom lip slightly jutting out. "It changes nothing. Has no use to me."

His magic had again soothed Kesst's stomach as he'd spoken, leaving behind more guilt, and envy, and wheeling disbelief. "Of course your looks have use to you," Kesst's slurred voice countered, as he frowned up at the healer's stubborn face. "If nothing else, *humans* care about looks more than anything. And you want a woman, don't you? A mate, and a son? Like every other orc alive?"

He couldn't quite hide the rising bitterness in his scent at that, because in all the ways he could match human women, or even surpass them, the sons were always the ultimate kick in the bollocks, weren't they? And sometimes Kesst truly felt like the only orc in the realm who didn't give a toss about finding a woman, and pumping out those sons. Who shuddered at even the *thought* of being permanently attached to a helpless, squalling little creature, who needed constant feeding and fussing and fretting over.

But to Kesst's genuine surprise, the healer shook his head, his mouth still set and grim. "No, I don't," he replied. "I don't care about any of that."

Huh. The healer didn't want a woman, or a son? At all? *Ever*?

It seemed utterly unthinkable—especially given the healer's equally unthinkable magic, which was so often passed down by blood—but there hadn't been the faintest twitch in that magic as he'd spoken, or on his frowning face. He truly meant that. Or thought he did.

"But your magic," Kesst said, his thin voice rising, and gods, why did he care, why was he even pushing this now, of all damned times? "Your gift. If you don't have a son, it could die with you, forever."

But the healer's magic still didn't change, his face just as stubborn as before. "And?" he said, his voice lower. "I do all I can to honour my gift, and share it with those in need. I don't owe the world another whole living *being*, who'll then be obligated to give *his* entire life to this, too."

To this. To moments like this, pouring his beautiful gift into a bloody babbling fool, who'd insulted his magic, and called him ugly, and carelessly thrown him straight into Kaugir and Skald's vicious, vengeful sights.

What good is he. Teach him a lesson. Cull him.

And suddenly Kesst just felt so cold, and so exhausted, and so empty. This damned healer, with his damned certainty, his damned infuriating nobility. His scent, his safety, his magic, *I don't care. I don't owe the world...*

"I'm sorry," Kesst whispered, his voice cracking, and he couldn't bear to look at the healer now, to see more of that pity in his eyes. "You shouldn't keep doing this for me. You could just toss me, you know. Into that thicket, maybe."

He was holding his prickling eyes very intently upon it, a particularly thorny patch of green slowly floating by, and he was truly, distantly astonished by the sound of the healer's chuckle. Low, warm, almost even... tolerant.

"I'm not tossing you into a thicket, Ash-Kai," he replied, with genuine-sounding amusement. "I'm healing you, and taking you home."

Oh. Oh. And gods, this healer, why was he doing this to him, what was happening to him? And why couldn't Kesst stop his nose from sniffing, or the water from escaping his eyes, streaking down his cheeks...

"You promise?" he whispered, humiliating, weak, *pathetic*—but he couldn't take it back, he was clinging to it, blinking desperately at the healer's eyes. "Please?"

And whatever it was, flickering like that in the healer's magic, on his face, Kesst couldn't have said. But that nod—that nod was a yes. Yes.

"Yes," the healer whispered back, and somehow, Kesst knew he meant it. "I promise."

5

The next thing Kesst knew was pain.

It was pain unlike anything he'd ever known, wrenching and wailing, wrecking every other thought in its wake. And Kesst could only seem to choke with it, writhe with it, feel it tear him apart, until—

"Fuck," breathed a low voice, a familiar voice, the healer's voice. "Hang on, Ash-Kai. Just—"

And suddenly, somehow, the pain was gone. And instead, Kesst's streaming-wet eyes were blinking up at the healer's scarred face, hovering close over him, with clear concern in his expressive dark eyes.

"Better?" the healer murmured, his voice quite possibly the most beautiful sound Kesst had ever heard—and he somehow nodded back, holding those eyes. And the healer was nodding too, his breath exhaling, his expression visibly relieved.

"Good," he said, and suddenly Kesst could feel a gentle hand slipping under his head, tilting it up, while something solid brushed against his lips. "Now drink for me, all right?"

Oh. It was a waterskin, the healer had even brought him

water, and Kesst obediently drank, swallowing the cool liquid in careful gulps. Feeling the healer's impossible magic in his belly as he drank, making sure it stayed calm and steady. Helping him. Saving him. Like he'd promised.

Kesst's thoughts were still swimming, scattering, as the waterskin drew away again, as that hand carefully set down his head. Onto something soft, the healer had put something *soft* beneath his head—and suddenly, blinking up at that already-familiar face, Kesst felt the most overwhelming, irrational urge to burst into tears. This was the most kindness anyone had shown him in so many moons, so many *years*—and it was surely the gods' own judgement that it was this healer, this stuffy, stick-up-the-rump healer, and...

"Should've tossed me," he heard his slurred voice say, his wet eyes still fixed to the healer's face. "Or at least let me suffer, just now. Sit back and laugh for a while, maybe."

The healer's worried eyes blinked, once—but then he shook his head, his lips twitching into a wry little smile. "I'm not about to let you suffer," he said firmly. "Let alone laugh at you."

Good gods, this healer, and Kesst felt his mouth convulsing, his eyes blinking even harder. "Pity me, then," his thick voice said. "That's even worse, I think."

The healer grimaced, and then—to Kesst's dulled distant astonishment—he nodded. "Right," he said, quiet. "I should have realized that, the other day. Sorry."

And wait. Why did he think he should have realized that, why was he apologizing to Kesst, when Kesst had been the one so unquestionably in the wrong? The one who'd mocked him to Skald and Kaugir, and helped throw a huge red target onto his back?

Kesst couldn't even seem to speak, suddenly, what with the heaviness and the guilt and exhaustion, the mess crowding his swirling skull. And the healer's hand had come to hover over his face, his brow creased with concern, his head shaking.

"Back to sleep for you, Ash-Kai," he murmured. "I'll keep a closer eye on your pain from now on, all right?"

Kesst should have protested, needed to protest, to say something, anything—but he was indeed already slipping away again, into dimming dizzying distance, into rising spinning dreams.

And while he often endured dark dreams, these were even worse than usual. Dreams of Ofnir's leering face, of Skald, of Kaugir. Dreams of his own weeping mother, his blank-eyed father, his laughing, pale-faced blood-brother. Of Grimarr frantically reaching for him, falling beneath Kaugir's huge axe, twitching and gasping in a pool of blood...

And of the healer. The healer carrying him, sliding that strong hand under his head, pouring water down his throat. The healer writhing beneath Skald's onslaught, his stubborn pride forever crushed beneath Skald's casual, careless cruelty. The healer barking back at Skald, risking himself, risking everything...

"No, I'm not waking him up," the fool snapped, reckless, hopeless. "He almost *died* two days ago, and he's still in critical condition. Now, if you want to discuss further, can we please take this out to—"

Skald's sudden bark felt like a handful of claws in Kesst's gut, like a looming dropping death-knell. "You *dare* refuse your captain's Left Hand, bewitcher?" his furious voice hissed, and rumbling beneath it were other voices too, all Skald's favourite Skai and Ash-Kai followers, and then the distinctive scrape of a sword. "I said, wake him!"

"And I said, no," the healer's voice countered, even more stubborn than before. "You could kill him!"

But no, no, it would be the healer dying now, it would be

him sprawled and convulsing in the pool of blood—but suddenly there were more voices spilling into Kesst's ringing ears, more chaos, pained-sounding shouts and groans, *Come at once, Efterar, Olarr was attacked whilst scouting, shall he...*

And when Kesst's hazy, gritty-feeling eyes next opened, the healer was still there. Still alive. His warm hand once again curling around the base of Kesst's skull, lifting his head, carefully pouring more cool water down his throat.

"Still alive," Kesst croaked at him, bewildered, once he'd finished swallowing, licking his dry lips. "Still here."

And he'd meant the healer, he wasn't supposed to be alive, Skald was culling him, *killing* him. But the healer's worried eyes had softened, his head nodding, his fingers slightly twitching against Kesst's head. "Still healing," he said, quiet. "But you're doing well. Better every day."

Kesst tried to shake his head, moving it pathetically against the healer's hand. "S'posed to be dead," he managed. "Culled."

And was that anger in the healer's eyes, in the magic Kesst could belatedly taste, swirling all through his head, his chest. "No," came his flat reply, impossibly sure of itself. "That's ridiculous. No one is culling me. Or you."

Oh. And staring up at his stubborn eyes, Kesst couldn't seem to find a way to argue. And he even felt himself relaxing again, almost as if he were safe again, as if...

"Should've tossed me," he said, and suddenly it felt crucially important that the healer understand this, realize this, take it all back. "Deserved it."

But the healer's eyes had softened again, his head shaking. "I'm healing you," he said. "I promised, remember?"

He'd promised. And if Kesst could have properly followed that, he might have laughed, or sobbed, or begged. But instead he just stared at it, marvelled at it, after all he'd said, all he'd done, he should be dead, he should be...

"Now stop thinking like that, Ash-Kai," the healer murmured, with astonishing gentleness in his voice. "And go back to sleep, all right?"

And lost in that moment, lost in the healer's eyes and his voice, Kesst could finally only nod, and obey.

6

The next time Kesst awoke, it was with his thoughts—his self—feeling far more coherent than before.

He was still alive. He could breathe. He could smell, he could see, he could feel all his limbs.

And—he blinked downward—he was tucked into a bed. There was a soft pillow beneath his head, and a heavy fur lying on top of him. And the bed was in a small, dank stone room, one he couldn't ever remember seeing before.

Kesst carefully sat up, sniffing at the air—from the scent of it, he was deep under Orc Mountain, likely in the area most preferred by the reclusive Ka-esh clan—and then he felt his breath catch at the close, distinctive scent of the healer. That sweet, impossibly powerful scent, not only here, near, in this room... but also *here*. Inside him.

Kesst's weak-feeling hand fluttered up to his chest, touching at where he could feel the healer's magic most—just below his collarbone, in the same place the crossbow bolt had impaled him. But instead of the ghastly wound—or even the scar—he'd expected, there was only smooth, even skin, with just the faintest twinge of tenderness beneath.

"Hey, careful with that," cut in a brusque voice—the healer's voice. And blinking toward it, Kesst found the healer standing up from beside another bed, in which another orc—Olarr, a huge and usually impressive Bautul warrior—appeared to be lying unconscious, his craggy face gone unnaturally pale, a thick binding wrapped around his chest.

Kesst blinked toward him for a moment, and then glanced around at the dank little room again, with its handful of brass beds, and its tiny crackling fire at the opposite end. Gods, it really was as though the healer had set up an actual *sickroom* of sorts, and how long had this even *been* here?

"Why are we buried down here in Ka-esh hell?" Kesst heard his voice croak, before he could stop it. "And Olarr isn't *dying*, is he?"

The healer was striding over toward Kesst now, his big body again clothed in a tunic and trousers, his hand clutching a bulging waterskin. "He'll be fine," he said, as he uncorked the waterskin, and held it out toward Kesst. "And Grimarr stuck me down here. Wanted to keep me well out of the way, I think."

Oh. Kesst blinked bemusedly at the healer's wry expression, at the steadiness in that big hand holding out the waterskin. Not touching him this time, not cradling his head and helping him drink, and for an instant Kesst almost felt disappointed, almost like—

Suddenly his own face and ears felt very warm, his gaze belatedly dropping—and he had to force his tingly fingers to snatch for the waterskin, and raise it to his mouth. This damned healer. Not only had he gone and fully healed what should have been a brutal, life-destroying wound, but he'd done it all with such impossible, unthinkable kindness. He'd made Kesst that promise, and he... he'd kept it.

"How are you feeling now?" the healer asked, once Kesst had finished drinking, and he'd taken back the waterskin again. "Any pain, or discomfort?"

The tips of Kesst's ears still felt unnaturally hot, and he touched at his chest again, more cautiously this time. "No," he said, and he couldn't quite hide the wonderment in his voice. "In truth, I feel frightfully good. Shouldn't I still be writhing in *some* modicum of excruciating agony right now?"

The healer's lips twitched, and for an instant Kesst could almost taste amusement in his scent. "I've been trying to keep down the pain for you," he replied, as his mouth pursed, and his gaze dropped to Kesst's chest. "Speaking of which, do you— do you mind if I touch you again?"

His voice had gone distinctly tentative, his eyes glancing uneasily at Kesst's face—and Kesst felt himself wincing as he recalled the reason for that question, that look. How he'd called the healer's magic *vile*, that day they'd first met. How he'd claimed he never wanted to taste it inside him again.

"Or not," the healer hurriedly said, and he'd even taken a step backwards, his hand clenching on the waterskin. "You'll still be all right now. I just won't be able to keep—"

He'd grimaced there, his eyes quickly darting away. And in return, something seemed to plummet, deep in Kesst's belly— and he saw his hands suddenly snapping up, and flailing toward the healer with highly betraying urgency.

"No, it's fine," he said, in a rush. "It's fine. I'll happily welcome your scent over an agonizing death any day. Obviously."

And curse him, he was making it even worse, because the healer's mouth twisted again, as if he'd tried to smile and utterly failed. And his step back toward Kesst was hesitant, almost reluctant, and the touch of his warm hand against the skin of Kesst's bare chest felt just the same, despite the sensation of that impossible magic unfurling deep and purposeful within.

"I'll try to make it quick," the healer said, his gaze still not meeting Kesst's. "Though I realize you'll probably never quite shake my scent now. I'm sorry."

Gods, could this healer *be* any more appalling, and Kesst felt his hands rubbing painfully at his face, his body shivering at the strength of that magic working away within him. Still fixing him. Helping him. Keeping his promise.

"It's really fine," he said thickly. "This is—very good of you. Again."

The healer gave a dismissive-looking shrug, but Kesst was almost sure he could taste relief in his magic, in the way it seemed to move with even more certainty, more ease, than before. Feeling so strong, so sweet, so... so *good*.

"It's no trouble," the healer replied, with another shrug. "Just doing what I can."

Doing what he could. And suddenly Kesst was drowning in the most bizarre urge to start weeping, or babbling, or frantically begging. This ridiculous noble healer, with his ridiculous damned innocence, with his impossibly beautiful magic. With his promise. His generosity. His kindness.

And damn it, it was too devastating, too absurd, too much to bear. And Kesst desperately needed to get away from this again, above this again, he was fine, he could do what he did best, he could—

"Well, in return, I'd be happy to do whatever I can for you," he heard himself say, as he attempted his best, most alluring smile up toward the healer's face. "How about a quick fuck, maybe? Or a suck? I have"—he let his tongue brush against his lips—"a *very* deep throat, you know."

The words seemed to ring between them, far too loud and brazen—and for a single, dangling instant, the healer snapped to sudden, perfect stillness. His body, his eyes, even his magic. All fully taut and frozen, and glimmering with shock, and disbelief, and...

And then he reeled backwards, his magic lashing almost

painfully away from Kesst, his head whipping back and forth, his long braid flaring out behind him. "*What*?" he demanded, far harsher than before. "No. *No*. Of course not."

Oh. And without that magic, without the healer's strangely fortifying touch, it felt like something had crumpled, deep inside Kesst's ribs. Something that flashed out the first full flare of pain, enough that his hand clutched against it, his body curling forward in the bed.

Gods, what the hell was wrong with him? Of course this healer didn't actually *want* anything like that from him. He was just doing his damned *job*, he'd already put up with far too much of Kesst's rubbish, and Kesst was... he was...

"Oh," he heard his voice say, sounding so small, so pathetically fragile. "Oh. Right. I—I see. I—"

He what? Gods, what? He'd thought a brilliant, noble orc like this would want him? *Him*? A pitiful, used-up plaything? Especially after everything Kesst had said to him? Everything he'd done?

And the miserable shamefulness just kept swinging, echoing, rattling deeper. Gods, Kesst hated this, hated himself, hated his entire damned *existence*—

When before him, the healer suddenly coughed, and stepped closer again. "Look, I—" he began, and when Kesst risked a wet-eyed glance upwards, the healer was rubbing at his face, his claws out, his scent flaring with inexplicable urgency.

"Look, you're very beautiful," he continued, in a rush. "And your scent is exquisite, and of course I'm very flattered. But I—I don't need payment, all right? And you're still *healing*, and"—he rubbed harder at his face—"and aren't you with that... that big Ash-Kai?"

Something far too powerful was washing over Kesst's body—*beautiful*, he'd said, *exquisite*, *flattered*—and it was enough that he heard himself bark a giddy, incredulous laugh. "With *who*?" his high-pitched voice asked. "Wait, with *Skald*?"

The healer was giving a helpless-looking shrug, his expression almost bewildered now. "You aren't?" he said thickly. "He came down here the other day with a whole band of hangers-on, railing on about how I needed to wake you up, so you could—well. But I sent him away, because you obviously weren't in any condition to do such things, so—"

He'd broken off there, but Kesst's mouth had fallen open, while sheer, barrelling horror surged through his chest. He hadn't dreamed that, about Skald coming down here, and asking for him? That had actually happened? This outrageous healer had *sent Skald away*?

"What the hell, healer," he breathed, his voice cracking. "That was real? You sent Skald away? *Skald*? When he came here wanting *me*?"

The healer was looking even more bewildered than before, but he nodded. "Yes?" he replied. "And why shouldn't I? He had no right to barge in here and start making demands of you, especially after—"

But Kesst was frantically flailing his hands again, and furiously shaking his head. "Stop, stop, stop," he snapped. "You cannot send Skald away like that. You cannot even look Skald in the *eyes*. If Skald comes to you and tells you to dance on your head, you *do* it!"

The healer blinked down at Kesst, and then folded his arms over his chest, his bottom lip jutting out. "That's ridiculous," he replied flatly. "You almost *died*, and where the hell was he then? And until you're fully healed again, no one is risking your health under *my* watch, in *my* damned sickroom!"

Kesst stared blankly up at the healer, while something new seemed to roil through his body. Some unholy blend of shock, and terror, and envy, and blatant downright *awe*.

"You clearly have a death wish, healer," he finally said, his voice very faint. "This is going to come back to wreck you, you know. It was already bad enough that I went and—"

And threw that target on your back, he'd been about to say—but now there was just so much guilt, so bitter and brittle, splintering in his gut. And that look in the healer's eyes said he already knew that, of course he already knew that, and he'd still kept doing all this? Still?

Suddenly Kesst couldn't bear to look at him anymore, and he painfully rubbed at his eyes, fought for something, anything, to say. "Well," he choked, "on a purely selfish level, I'm very grateful that you healed me before you went off and got yourself slaughtered and fed to the crows, at least."

And gods, it was the worst joke, the worst thing to say, again—but before he could fumble for yet another useless apology, he heard the healer... *laugh*? The sound low and indulgent, firing impossible licks of heat all the way up Kesst's too-stiff spine.

"Me, too," his voice replied, slicing so soft and deep into Kesst's belly, into his soul. "And look, don't worry about that swine, all right? I'm not fussed over some loud overgrown lout barking at me."

It was enough to snap Kesst's face up again, exposing his sheer disbelief, his still-wet eyes. "Unbelievable," his thick voice said. "You're a reckless, ruinous *menace*, healer. I give it one more day, at most, before I'm weeping over your dead body."

But the healer was still smiling—*smiling!*—and gods, the warmth in his scent, the way it almost tasted like...

"Weeping, huh?" he replied, even softer, arching a thick black brow toward Kesst. And suddenly heat was swarming Kesst's face, his tooth biting awkwardly at his lip, his lashes fluttering like he was some startled, staring innocent.

And oh, the healer's face had slightly flushed too, his gaze finally angling away, breaking the rising tension between them.

And again, there was the overwhelming urge to start babbling, or perhaps pleading. To keep pushing this, even, seeing how far he could take it, because the longing was suddenly so strong he felt faint. Gods, how would it feel to touch a magnificent doomed angel like this, to suck out his seed, to make him moan and beg for more...

But instead Kesst only sat there, breathing hard, while the heat kept prickling at his face. Until the healer finally cleared his throat, and shifted on his feet.

"You should probably get some more rest," he said, his voice gruff. "Do you mind if I put you out again for a while? Though I'll need to touch you again, if that's—"

But Kesst was staring at him again, pleading at him again, needing him again. "Yes, of course, whatever you like," he heard his flustered voice say. "And you really don't need to keep asking, I really don't mind, I..."

I like it, he'd been about to blurt out, *I like you*. And even if he hadn't finished it, that was surely more comprehension, more relief, in the healer's too-expressive eyes.

"Good," he murmured, as his hand slowly slid down to Kesst's head, easing with breathtaking gentleness against his hair. "Then lie down, will you?"

And oh, Kesst could only nod, obey, drink up that beautiful touch, those beautiful eyes. And that was all he knew as he drifted away again, into the safe, soft sweet darkness.

7

T o Kesst's genuine amazement, the healer survived through the next day, and the next, and the next.

It certainly helped that Grimarr had stuck him well out of Kaugir and Skald's way down here, and that he'd made his own personal endorsement of the healer very, very clear. Grimarr had also marched down a steady rotation of previously valuable fighters who'd been suffering from various ailments—Ezog with his blown-out knee, Sigarr with his bad shoulder, Thorvald with his chronic shortness of breath—and had apparently made large public to-dos over their miraculous recoveries.

And it *was* miraculous, Kesst could readily admit now. A gift. And rather than the creeping discomfort and abject boredom he ought to have felt upon being stuck in Ka-esh hell for days on end, he'd found himself spending bizarre amounts of time just lying there in his bed, and watching the healer work. Tasting his magic, drinking up his scent, listening to him speak.

And in it, Kesst had learned rather a lot about his doomed, shockingly gifted saviour. The healer was often blunt and curt, but never cruel. He rarely responded to short tempers or personal attacks, but instead ignored them, and said only what needed to be said. And even when faced with some of the most terrifying orcs Kesst knew—most of them in various states of rage, pain, or humiliation—he remained his same stubborn self, betraying not even the faintest trace of intimidation or fear.

"No, you can't go back to the arena yet," the healer was currently snapping at Silfast, a huge, hairy Bautul fighter who was pooling large quantities of fresh blood onto the floor. "And if you even try, I will knock you out, and keep you down here for a *week*."

Silfast's snarled, shouting reply was nearly enough to make Kesst's hair stand on end—but the healer just shrugged, and raised his hand to Silfast's head. And Kesst couldn't help a choked, genuine laugh as Silfast's eyes promptly rolled back, and he collapsed onto the bed behind him with a deeply satisfying *thunk*.

At the sound of Kesst's laugh, the healer shot a wry glance over his shoulder toward him—and then, much to Kesst's secret delight, he turned and strode over, too. As he so often did whenever Kesst laughed or spoke, though since that first day, he'd been nothing but strictly professional. Speaking to Kesst only of wounds and rest and healing, and whatever ungrateful orc was currently giving him the most grief.

"How are you feeling today?" he asked now, as his big hand settled to Kesst's head—without asking, Kesst's gratified brain pointed out—where it perhaps even lingered a little before pulling away again. "Any pain?"

"Still no, healer," Kesst replied, fluttering his lashes as he smiled up at the healer's face. "As you probably already knew, being the devious master magician that you are."

He was rewarded by a faint but unmistakable flush, stealing up the healer's cheeks. "That's a bit rich for *you* to say," he countered, his bottom lip slightly jutting out. "You don't think I haven't noticed the old magic all over you too, Ash-Kai?"

He softened that highly unnerving statement with a gentle brush of his hand against Kesst's bare chest, his magic flaring out with such deep, delicious familiarity—and Kesst covered his reflexive gasp with a cough, and a hopefully flippant toss of his hair over his shoulder.

"It's Kesst," he corrected the healer, purposely sidestepping that question about his magic. "My name. You might as well start using it, since I essentially owe you my entire *existence* right now."

The healer snorted, gave another wry shake of his head. "You don't owe me anything," he said firmly. "And I have a name too, you know."

Right. The warmth was pooling and shuddering, curling up in the ongoing tendrils of that beautiful magic, in the meaning behind those words. *I have a name too.*

Efterar, was the healer's name. Efterar. And he wanted Kesst—*Kesst!*—to use it.

"Your name is preposterous," Kesst informed him, far louder and faster than he meant. "I mean, was your father a five-hundred-year-old swamp-dweller who never learned common-tongue? Because I guarantee you, it wasn't your poor mother who saddled you with that thing."

The healer—*Efterar*—was looking rather taken aback, and far, far too late, Kesst winced, and snapped his fool mouth closed. "I mean," he said, squeezing his eyes shut, "it's very—unique. Just—an unusual choice, for an orc who doesn't even speak Aelakesh."

But curse him, that was even worse, what the hell was his damned mouth *saying*—until a mortified peek up at the healer found him exhaling, and... shrugging?

"My father didn't live long enough to teach me his

language," he replied, quiet. "You could maybe call me Eft, if that's any better."

And gods, this healer, because Kesst's hard, gulping swallow was surely audible, and visible, no doubt screaming its guilt toward that magic still working away inside him. Still healing him with so much kindness, even now. Still keeping that promise.

"Then Eft it is," Kesst belatedly said, with a failed attempt at a bracing smile. "A very strong and straightforward name, just like you. And look, if you'd ever like to learn more Aelakesh, I'd be happy to try and teach you—though I'll warn you, I'm likely to be just as dreadful at it as I am at everything else. Cocksucking and flattery excluded, of course."

The healer—Eft—blinked, and then betrayed a brief, choked-sounding chuckle, even as his cheeks noticeably flushed again. "Nonsense, Kesst," he said, low. "I'd be honoured to have you teach me. And no more putting down my patients in my sickroom, all right? Especially the only one who actually does as I tell him."

And oh, Kesst's swelling heart, his swelling *cock*, twitching to life in his trousers. And damn it, but the healer knew it, he saw it, his eyes widening—and suddenly he'd lurched fully away, whipping his magic along behind him. But before it had gone, Kesst could have sworn there'd been something else in it, something warm and fluid and deep. Something... *hungry*.

And Kesst wanted it back, he needed it back, so much it ached. Enough that he felt himself clearing his throat, the impulse surging, escaping...

"You know, you can tell me what to do anytime, Eft," he heard himself murmur, husky and hot. "Anything you want."

And had he wanted Eft to twitch and stare like that... he had, he *had*. And Eft's eyes on him suddenly looked almost as ravenous as Kesst felt, and he felt his tongue brush his lips, his mouth opening to speak, to say...

"Ach, brothers," broke in a familiar, thoroughly ill-timed voice, and Kesst huffed an irritated sigh as he glanced toward the door. It was Grimarr, his face hard and blank, his hand clutching the sword-hilt at his side. And between that tone in his voice, and the look on his face, Kesst felt his bubbling warmth draining away all at once, leaving something cold and slimy behind.

"My father and Skald are hosting a revel in the Ash-Kai common-room," Grimarr said, his voice just as hard as his face. "And they have commanded you both to come and show yourselves. At once."

8

K esst stared at Grimarr for a long, silent moment, while his heart suddenly began beating a sickening pulse in his chest. A revel. Commanded. At once.

"But I'm still wounded," he protested, which perhaps wasn't quite as true as it had been, but he could still cling to it, damn it. "And Eft's far too busy. Dealing with all the ungrateful louts *you* keep sending him, I might add."

Grimarr betrayed a pained-looking grimace, and then shook his head, his eyes dark. "I have already gained you five days' reprieve, brother," he said, quiet. "I cannot risk pushing this further, without drawing more of their ire toward you. Unless"—he grimaced again as he glanced between Kesst and Eft, his gaze oddly sharpening on how Eft's hand had somehow come to rest against Kesst's shoulder—"you might rather wish to leave the mountain together for a spell, mayhap. I can claim I could not find you, grant you a few days' start—"

Kesst's thoughts were wildly churning now, racing down too many messy paths at once. How many times had Grimarr already dealt with his father and Skald on their behalf? How much fallout would Grimarr face if Kesst and Eft both up and

vanished, under his watch? Would it destroy whatever nefar-
ious plots Grimarr had clearly been busily hatching of late?

And most crucial of all, surely Eft would never actually run
away with Kesst, straight into the middle of a *war*? Just to
escape a single stupid *party*?

Suddenly Kesst couldn't bear to look at Eft, to see what he
might think of all this—and he belatedly lurched out of bed,
and yanked up his saggy, grimy-feeling trousers. "Of course
we'll come," he said, as he stalked past Eft, and fixed Grimarr
with his coldest smile. "I *love* parties. Ready whenever you are,
brother."

Grimarr didn't bother smiling back, but just nodded,
waiting until Eft finally came over, too. And Kesst still couldn't
seem to look at Eft as they followed Grimarr out the door, and
up the dank narrow corridor. It was the first time Kesst had
walked any actual distance since his injury, and he found
himself absurdly grateful for the gentle brush of Eft's hand
against his back, his impossible magic now unfurling downwards, sending strength to his legs and feet.

"So what's the occasion, then?" Kesst said to Grimarr's stiff
shoulders, after a few moments of too-taut silence. "Another
raid? Or did your father steal away another woman again?"

Grimarr made a sound that might have been a laugh, but
wasn't. "Ach, he sought to do both," he replied, his voice very
even, though his hand was still gripped tight to his sword-hilt.
"In Varrahan. He raided the home of the magistrate, and meant
to bring back his wife. To surprise me, he said. To gain me a
son. But she…"

Grimarr didn't need to finish, and Kesst made a similar
laughing sound, cold and empty. "I hope it was quick, at least?"
he said, as lightly as he could. "The magistrate's dead too, I
presume?"

Kesst still couldn't seem to look at Eft beside him, but he
could taste the sudden flare of disbelief in his still-working

magic, followed by a surge of sustained, simmering anger. Strong enough that Kesst gripped at Eft's arm, letting his still-stubby claws dig in, while he kept watching Grimarr's shoulders, waiting.

"Ach," Grimarr finally said, with a heavy sigh. "And their house emptied of goods and ale, and then burnt, whilst all the town grieves and rages against us. Thus... this *revel*."

Oh. How lovely, and how damned typical, a party to celebrate destroying gods knew how many helpless humans' lives. And even more typical, by throwing said party in the Ash-Kai common-room, Kaugir and Skald would also ensure that only their favoured orcs—namely, the Ash-Kai and Skai—could even partake of the short-lived fruits of their labours.

"And your father's mood?" Kesst asked Grimarr, his voice very thin. "And Skald's?"

"Very jolly," said Grimarr, just as thin. "Very... hungry."

This assessment proved unnervingly apt, Kesst soon discovered, as he and Eft followed Grimarr into the loud, chaotic Ash-Kai common-room. It wasn't a large room to begin with, but it currently felt stuffed to bursting with scents and shouting and laughter, with dozens of Skai and Ash-Kai orcs revelling in their victories.

And while Kesst certainly wasn't opposed to a good rioting party, he could indeed already feel the distinctive edge on this one. The way Kaugir, lounging at the front of the room on a large bench—his de facto throne—was sweeping his beady eyes over the assembled revellers, his dark-stained scimitar lying unsheathed in his lap. While beside him, Skald was fully bared, his head thrown back as he laughed, his massive body streaked all over with dried red blood. And before him, another orc—Benkt, a smaller Ash-Kai—was kneeling, working over his groin with palpable effort, while Skald blatantly ignored him, and again broke into riotous laughter at whatever Kaugir had just said.

Kesst had found himself hesitating near the door, his eyes reflexively angling toward Eft, who had halted beside him. And who, predictably, was making no attempt to conceal his obvious contempt toward this entire little scene, his brow darkly furrowed, his lip curling with distaste.

Thankfully, Grimarr's big body before them was strategically blocking Eft from Skald's view, and Kesst could see Grimarr working to bring the smile to his mouth, before clapping a nearby Alfrik on the shoulder, and congratulating him on his day's gain. And then moving steadily forward through the room, with a barely perceptible glance back toward Kesst and Eft that was very clearly an order, all the same. *Follow me.*

But Kesst was already doing it, and smiling, too—one did not enter a gathering like this without first paying one's respects to one's captain—at least, until he realized that Eft had made no move to join them, and the touch of his magic had dropped from Kesst's back. Not only that, but Eft was viciously glowering at the orc—Skarpi—who'd just bumped into him, and sloshed his drink onto his tunic.

"This way," Kesst hissed, gripping Eft's arm again, and herding him around Skarpi. "And drop the death glare, for the love of the gods."

Eft didn't resist, but his eyes on Kesst were still stubborn, and maybe confused, too. "Why?" he muttered back. "It *reeks* in here. And I have no interest in—"

Kesst dug his claws deeper, and kept his own smile pinned to his face. "Because," he said, through gritted teeth. "We don't want you to *die* today!"

Eft blinked at him, clearly nonplussed once again—and for perhaps the first time, it fully occurred to Kesst just how ingrained these little games, these small cruelties and injustices, had become in his own awareness, his own existence. One always paid respects to Kaugir, before all else. One always simpered and smiled, never showing anger or weariness or disgust. One never risked speaking one's true thoughts, because one might very quickly become an example, an entertainment, for the rest of the hungry mob.

And because all the other orcs were doing exactly the same, you never quite knew where you stood among them. You never quite knew which ones would heartily laugh as your entrails were carved out, or which ones would furtively try to help you. You had ideas, of course, hints and scents and glances—but when it came down to it, you could never truly be sure.

And as Kesst watched Grimarr so smoothly play the game in front of them, smiling, laughing, speaking praises and congratulations, he suddenly just felt cold, and sick, and empty. Grimarr was trying, Kesst knew, he'd been trying for years— but that uncertainty had always been there, undermining him, impeding him. Which orcs were his, and which were his father's? How many orcs would ultimately take his side, and join him in unseating their all-powerful captain, who had ruled over them for most of their lives? And how many orcs would turn on Grimarr, and seek to kill him—and surely all his friends and supporters—before the next sunrise?

And worst of all, how much more misery and bloodshed would that bring? How many more orcs would die in the midst of a full-on mutiny? Would it be the end of their kind, and their home? Forever?

Kesst had briefly stopped moving, and he felt himself dragging in breath, fighting to calm his churning stomach—when he again felt that gentle, familiar hand, settling against his back. While Eft's magic again twined deep inside him, stroking at his stomach, soothing it again.

Damn, it was good, and Kesst couldn't seem to stop himself from leaning into that touch, into Eft's solid body beside him. Into how Eft was shifting even closer too, almost *embracing* him, good gods, his breath warm on Kesst's cheek.

"I'll try," he murmured, very quiet. "Is this better?"

This. And maybe he meant Kesst's stomach, which was indeed greatly improved, or—Kesst twitched—maybe he meant his own smile. Which was a ghastly, painted-on, sharp-toothed grimace, horribly contorting his face, and Kesst winced at the sight, even as he betrayed a bark of bright, genuine laughter.

"That is *not* better," he countered, under his breath. "You've just become the most terrifying orc in this room, you menace. Honestly, are you *trying* to get yourself killed?"

Eft's appalling grin had abruptly warmed, softened, becoming something that made Kesst's heart skip a beat. His own smile curving with genuine warmth, too—and at that inopportune moment, Grimarr halted in front of his father and Skald, and bent into the usual low bow, his fist over his heart. Revealing Kesst and Eft behind him, and Kesst hurriedly bowed too, desperately fighting to ignore the weight of Kaugir and Skald's combined gazes upon him.

"Ach, what trickery is this?" Skald's harsh voice said as Kesst arose, his big hands roughly shoving a red-faced Benkt off to the side. "Our pretty wench yet lives! I was sure"—his eyes sharpened as he glanced at Eft—"you had died, to keep spurning your betters as you have. It has been what, five days, Captain, since he has come to serve us?"

Kesst attempted his most ingratiating smile down toward Skald, and again fervently sought to ignore the heaviness of Kaugir's eyes upon him, the tension in Eft's body beside him. "I assure you, it's been the most *excruciating* wait," he said to Skald, flipping his hair over his shoulder. "Of course, I only didn't want to risk disappointing you with my frightful indisposition, so I've been—"

"Getting on his knees for our useless new bewitcher, I ken," cut in Kaugir's deep voice, his heavy gaze now intent on Eft. "Who has not yet honoured his betters, ach?"

Kesst could feel the faint twist of Eft's magic inside him—

wait, was Eft *still* touching him?—and thankfully Grimarr had shifted on his feet, stepping a little closer. "Our gifted Ash-Kai healer is new to the mountain, and yet learns our ways," he said, with a meaningful glance toward Eft, and another slow, purposeful bow toward his father. "It is done thus, ach?"

Eft stiffly obliged, keeping his gaze low as he bowed, his other hand still on Kesst's back. And Kesst could have groaned at the sight of it, at the way Skald's eyes had flicked to Eft's hand, and instantly narrowed. And at the way he himself should have swiftly stepped away from Eft, should have knocked away the sheer wheeling peril in his touch, but some-how... couldn't.

"Ach, our new *bewitcher*," Skald sneered. "Who has dared, Captain, to disobey me, and dishonour me. Who refused to grant me *my* wench, on my command!"

Grimarr had opened his mouth to speak again, but his father forestalled it with a curt, forceful slap of his scimitar against Grimarr's torso. "And how did this weakling bewitcher seek to make amends for this sin against you?" Kaugir drawled at Skald. "Did he offer you his shameful innocence, mayhap? Or did he offer to show you his... *healing*?"

This was said with a meaningful little smirk toward Skald, who was looking speculative now, a vicious grin curling at his mouth. "No, this bewitcher offered *naught* to make amends to me," he replied coldly, as he dropped his hand to his still-wet, still-bared prick, and dragged a sharp claw down the length of it, leaving a swelling line of red behind. "Though I ken now he shall, ach? With his mouth, mayhap. And should he fail..."

His hand was reaching sideways, toying with the hilt of his own bloodstained scimitar, which was lying on the bench beside him. And Kesst was suddenly, viscerally aware of the slowly quieting room, of the increasingly watchful audience around them. Of the dark, dizzying danger that was hovering in this moment, so close, so ready to strike...

And the danger wasn't only in Skald and Kaugir's taunting, leering, waiting eyes, but also in the realization that Grimarr couldn't risk sparking that mutiny here, not in a room of drunken, rioting, outwardly loyal orcs, all pinned firmly under Kaugir's thumb. And worst of all, the danger was here in the hard press of Eft's hand to Kesst's back, and the reeling, over-powering *rage* that was now flooding deep into Kesst's skin. Saying no, Eft would not kneel for Skald, he would never, *never*.

And for that, he would die.

The sheer barrelling terror was suddenly screeching, wracking through Kesst's chest—and somehow he lurched forward, away from Eft's comfort and his fury, and into the wolf's waiting mouth. Or rather, between his sprawled, waiting thighs.

"Really, Skald?" Kesst's voice demanded, with as much high-pitched disbelief as it could possibly muster. "I haven't seen you for five whole days, and now you're here offering your favours to him? *Him*?!"

He cast his most disdainful glance back toward Eft, and then dismissed him altogether with a flippant toss of his hair over his shoulder. "That healer is *hideous*," he informed Skald. "And he *reeks*, and clearly has no manners, and no sense. It's no damned wonder he hasn't been touched before—I mean, *really*—and now you're just going to grant him our Left Hand's priceless seed? Just like that?"

He snapped his fingers in front of Skald's face, and then put his hands to his hips, and assumed his best, sultriest pout. "I have been trapped down in Ka-esh hell with this stuffy, stodgy, stubborn lout for *five endless days*," he continued, "doing all my very best healing for you, so I could come up here and properly serve you! Don't I deserve *some* kind of credit for that? And if you give my rewards to *him* instead, I shall be very, *very* vexed, Skald!"

Skald was watching, he was listening, that surely wasn't

anger glimmering in his eyes, was it?—so Kesst gave a ridiculous stamp of his foot, another haughty toss of his head. "Your next load is *mine*, you big infuriating tease," he announced imperiously, stepping even closer, almost near enough to touch. "No matter *what* I need to do to get it!"

And yes, yes, it was working, because Skald's hand had finally released his scimitar, and that was surely amusement—and hunger—crackling in his eyes. And next to him, Kaugir had even given an indulgent laugh, elbowing Skald in the side as he downed his goblet.

"Ach, Skald, you shall not bear your silly, spoilt wench making such a fuss, shall you?" he said. "He needs some reminding of his place, I ken."

The bitterness choked in Kesst's throat, but he kept that thwarted look on his face, that lofty tilt to his chin. And yes, Skald's eyes were heavy-lidded now, leering up and down Kesst's too-close form, while his blood-streaked hand dropped to stroke up the other waiting, leaking weapon, hovering at his groin.

"Ach, then kneel for me, foolish wench," he growled at Kesst. "And show me how sweetly you can beg."

9

————

Kesst spent the rest of the day moaning and pleading in the Ash-Kai common-room, freely offering Skald everything he damn well wanted from him. His pleasure, his pain, his hunger, his humiliation.

It didn't stop until the party had finally quieted, and Skald had fallen asleep on the bench, snoring loudly toward the ceiling. Kaugir had thankfully left with his Skai hangers-on by that point, but Grimarr was still there, leaning back against the nearest wall, gazing blankly at the ceiling. And when he saw Kesst staggering toward the door, he lurched over to walk beside him, his hand steadying Kesst's elbow, his eyes darkening as they flicked up and down his bared form.

"Ach, brother," he said, under his breath, once they were a good distance down the corridor again. "You will go have Efterar look at you, ach?"

Kesst couldn't suppress his grimace, the hard swallow of his throat. "Eft didn't stick around long in there," he said, his voice a croak. "Did he?"

"No," Grimarr said, with a sigh. "In truth, I sent him away, soon after you went to Skald. He is not one to hide his thoughts, or hold his tongue, ach?"

No, no he wasn't, and Kesst felt the strangest, most alarming urge to start shouting, or sobbing. "You need to do something," he hissed at Grimarr, his voice cracking. "Something more. You were right, Eft's healing is a damned *miracle*, and we were just going to sit there and watch while they made a mockery of him, and probably *killed* him?!"

Grimarr was rubbing his hand against his face, his claws out, his breath exhaling. "I would have sought to find another way," he said, very quiet. "I did not ken Efterar had already drawn their ire thus, else I should never have brought him before them. So I thank you, brother, for your quick mind in this. Your bravery."

Ha. Kesst's bravery. As if he wasn't quite possibly the greatest coward in the mountain. As if he hadn't just thrown himself at one of the most vile orcs alive, and—yes, even now—found *pleasure* in it.

And worst of all, as if he hadn't borne any blame in this, when he should have thought to warn Grimarr. He should have told him the truth about how he'd helped throw that target on Eft's back. Maybe—maybe he should have even told Eft to take that offer to run.

"And I am doing all I can, ach?" Grimarr's voice continued, even quieter. "With Ofnir dead, we are this much closer, but Skald..."

But Skald. Huge, treacherous, highly unpredictable, quick to rage and to strike. Not only that, but he was a spectacular warrior, who particularly excelled in single combat, and whose entire existence as Left Hand depended on his protection of his equally treacherous captain. And if it came down to a full-on battle between Grimarr and his father, Skald would do everything within his power to utterly destroy Grimarr, without a second thought.

"Then get rid of Skald," Kesst hissed back, his own voice barely audible. "As fast as possible, damn it!"

Grimarr groaned and rubbed his face again, his shoulders sagging. "You ken I have not sought to gain this?" he breathed. "He does not bathe, so he cannot be drowned. He will not enter a pitched battle, so he cannot be found by a stray sword. Arrows and blades and poisons betray the scents of their wielder, and any trickery upon this will surely draw too many eyes toward us. I have searched for a human assassin to hire, but none shall speak to us—mayhap wise, for my father should next hunt him down and kill *him*, also. I cannot even seek to build a wedge between my father and Skald, for he scarce leaves Skald's side, and listens to *naught* that I speak! It is only now that I—"

Grimarr's voice halted there, but it had already gone sharp and furious, surely risking far more than was prudent—and he'd clearly realized that, too, because he abruptly stopped walking, and slammed the flat of his hand into the nearest wall. "I have drunk too much," he said, louder than before, his eyes darting uneasily around the corridor. "I know not what I speak of. We both need rest, brother."

With that, he spun and stalked off, his shoulders hunched, his hand gripped at his scimitar. And Kesst suddenly felt his own rage pooling away as he watched, leaving only that dark, bitter sickness behind. That... dread.

Because yes, he'd managed to waylay Skald today—but there were so, so many more days. And Eft's responses today hadn't helped the situation, not in the least—and Skald certainly wouldn't forget that, either. No matter how many stupid little tantrums Kesst threw. No matter what price he paid.

But gods, what possible answers were there? Try to drag Eft out of the mountain, into the middle of a deadly war? Abandon his own home, and everything he knew? Or maybe—something twisted hard in Kesst's gut—maybe it would be best to firmly shove Eft away, distance himself from him forever, in hopes that Skald might somehow, someday, forget him?

And as he hauled himself off to the grimy, half-empty baths, washing himself up as best he could, his despair only seemed to seep colder, deeper. Gods, he'd fucked this up. All the things he'd said, all the things he'd done. Not just today, but for years, and years, and years.

That orc is hideous. And he reeks, and clearly has no manners, and no sense. It's no wonder he hasn't been touched before. Do whatever you want with him. Does it look like I care? I love the taste of his blood on you. More, harder, please, whatever you want.

And there was the whisper, not new, that perhaps it would be easiest to slip under the water, once and for all. To just make it stop, to relent to the justice he so desperately deserved.

But he was too selfish, too damned self-absorbed, to even manage that much. And instead, he trudged his still-bared, dripping-wet body all the way back down to Ka-esh hell. To that dank little sickroom. To... Eft.

And gods, what would Eft say now. What would he look like, smell like. Would he mock Kesst, judge him, reject him? Would he be hurt and betrayed? Would he refuse to speak to him, or even to heal him, after everything Kesst had said about him? Again?

But when Kesst hesitated in the sickroom doorway, Eft's head snapped up, from where he'd been working over an unconscious-looking Drafli, one of Grimarr's shadows—and then he instantly lurched over. Not stopping, not even hesitating, as he pressed both his hands to Kesst's bare chest, his magic unfurling in a furious, beautiful rush of heat.

"Gods damn it, Kesst," he hissed, his voice cracking, his eyes unnervingly bright. "What the *fuck*."

There was pure, bristling rage in his scent now, in his touch, in his magic—but that touch still didn't hesitate, not for an instant. And oh, one big warm hand was even sliding up Kesst's chest, caressing slow and purposeful to the multiple fresh bites on his neck, while the magic kept flaring out in its wake.

Kesst's cursed throat swallowed hard against the heat of Eft's hand, and in response it slid even closer, the strength of its palm firm and impossibly, alarmingly reassuring. "These will *not* scar," Eft growled, with a fervour that felt entirely unfounded. "I swear to you, Kesst."

And suddenly Kesst was so, so close to weeping, to breaking, to ruining everything—and even as his nose betrayed a pathetic little sniff, he managed a huff, and a cool, practiced smile. "You don't need to worry about it," he replied, his voice thin. "I'll be fine. I always am. I *loved* it."

But that was surely the wrong thing to say, flaring even more fury into Eft's still-caressing hands, into the sharp sweep of his eyes up and down Kesst's bared form. "No," he snapped back. "Go. Lie down. *Now.*"

But Kesst had betrayed a faint, unmistakable flinch—perhaps at Eft's command, or his tone, or his anger, or all of it—and in response, Eft instantly reeled back from him, shaking his head, rubbing his hands at his mouth. His magic snapping away too, and suddenly Kesst wanted to weep again, or to shout again, to throw all his sickening guilt straight into Eft's face...

"Happy to oblige," he heard his voice say, as he walked past Eft to his usual bed, holding his head high, keeping his steps as even as he could, perhaps even swaying his bare hips a little. "Because I meant it, you know, when I said you can tell me what to do. Because you can. Because I *like* it."

Kesst could feel Eft's eyes on him, but he suddenly couldn't bear to look back, and instead flopped face-down on the bed, biting off his resulting grunt of pain. "I like it," he said again, harder this time, burying his eyes in his forearm. "I like big powerful orcs like you, and like Skald. I like you bossing me around, and looking at me, and paying attention to me, and touching me. I like you *wanting* me."

And gods, he was really saying all this, driving himself deeper, so deep he'd never get out again—and he could feel Eft still standing there, watching him, surely judging him like he deserved, once and for all.

"And I love you fucking me most of all," Kesst made himself continue, his voice even harder than before. "I'm such a fucking size queen, always have been, always will be. Skald's is the fattest in the whole mountain, you know, so of course I'm all over that, any damned time he wants. Then there's Simon, one of the least vile Skai, who's even longer, and nearly as thick— that length is life-changing, feeling it rearrange your insides like that—but he won't give it to me anymore because Skald gets threatened, you know? And have you seen Grimarr's yet, it's very, *very* nice, and I'd be on that every day if he'd let me. But he won't either, so I'm still stuck with Skald, and I know he's vile but I'll still do anything he wants, *anything.*"

By the end of it, it felt like his own voice was choking him, drowning him in the bitter, horrifying shamefulness of its truth. Because it had all been true, every single sordid word of it, and now Eft would finally leave him, would walk away forever, and...

"Do you mind if I touch you again, then, to address some of this?" came Eft's voice, quiet. "Is there anywhere you'd rather I didn't?"

He indeed hadn't quite touched Kesst, but that was still a very light, very tentative brush of magic against his bare shoulder. And Kesst's shivering gasp betrayed even more of his towering shame, his taint, his weak, wretched guilt.

"I told you, I don't care," he gritted out, into the bed. "Do whatever the hell you want."

He could hear Eft's exhale, could feel it on his skin. Followed by the warm touch of Eft's hand, so careful, so gentle, as his fingers spread wide against Kesst's upper back, his magic again spiralling familiar and deep.

It focused on Kesst's original chest wound first, on where there was indeed a renewed throbbing pain, no doubt thanks to Skald's rough, careless handling. And as Eft kept working, Kesst could almost taste his anger rising again, threading through his magic—but that hand just kept staying, kept fixing, kept healing. Until the pain in Kesst's chest had finally faded altogether, and the magic flicked to what was likely the worst bruise, curling around his neck.

And again, it was so pathetic, and so shameful, but Kesst still found himself sinking into it, settling, relaxing. His frantic, miserable thoughts slowly quieting, calming, as the pain kept fading, flickering away. As Eft moved his way down his body, steady and methodical, with still no censure, and no judgement.

"Why are you still doing this," Kesst finally mumbled, into his arm. "You know I don't deserve this. I'm a—"

"Kesst," Eft cut in, his magic flaring, his voice shuddering into Kesst's bones. "Enough of that, all right? You deserve all the help I can give you. And I want to help. However I can."

Kesst choked a disbelieving laugh, shaking his head into his arm. "That's such a load of rubbish," he bit out. "Did you not *hear* what I called you up there? I said you were hideous, and stuffy, and stodgy, and stubborn, and smelly. That you have no manners, and no sense. That it was no *wonder* you'd never been touched before!"

But to Kesst's astonishment, that might have actually been a hint of a wry chuckle, shuddering Eft's touch against him. "Well, luckily, I already knew you thought all that about me," he replied. "So it wasn't as though I was shocked, all right?"

Gods, this *healer*, because suddenly something had viciously wrenched in Kesst's belly, while his eyes prickled painfully into his arm. "But you know," he whispered back, before he could possibly stop it, "I didn't—I don't mean *all* of it. Don't think all that about you."

His face was burning against his arm, his throat swallowing, and it was so mortifying, so fucking ridiculous—but Eft just kept touching him, healing him, keeping that promise.

"Is that so?" Eft asked, his voice far lighter than it had any right to be. "Let me guess, then. You definitely still think I'm stodgy and stuffy, right? And stubborn?"

Kesst heard himself betray a muffled huff, but couldn't otherwise speak, and Eft's fingers drummed a little against him. "And I don't have much time for manners, that's true," he continued. "Or sense, apparently, either, based on how I escalated things up there today."

His voice had lowered at that part, his fingers spreading wider against Kesst's back, his magic now curling against one of the scrapes Skald's claws had made. "I'm truly sorry about that, by the way," he added, his voice even lower. "I'm sorry you had to step in to cover for my stupidity. It was very, very generous of you, and I won't forget it. Thank you."

Kesst couldn't speak now, just shaking his head, fighting to swallow over the clog in his throat. And Eft's hand slid up and down his back a little, perhaps not even healing now, but just caressing, fluttering his magic deep within. "And I won't ever put you at risk like that again, either," he whispered. "I promise, Kesst."

Curse this healer, making these cursed promises again, and reinforcing them with that hard purpose in his voice, with the stunning reassurance of his magic and his touch. This cursed healer, making Kesst believe him, making Kesst long for him, like he'd never longed for anything in his life.

"Definitely still no sense, though," Kesst somehow made his hoarse voice reply. "And no sense of self-preservation, either. Or taste."

And oh, Eft was still just stroking him like that, his magic wheeling a little wider, a little further downwards. "Hey," he murmured, as that hand slid even lower, very close to the curve of Kesst's bare arse. "I may not be much to look at—or smell—but I'll have you know, I have *excellent* taste."

And he was doing it again, Kesst was dangerously close to weeping again, shaking his head against his arm. "Rubbish again, Eft," he breathed. "To *all* of that."

Eft's touch against him had stilled, surely taking that for what it was—for an admission, blatant and shameful, that Kesst *did* like looking at him, and smelling him, and feeling him like this. Feeling this... ease. This... safety.

But then Eft cleared his throat, something shifting in his magic, in his touch. "Are you sure you want me to keep going?" he said, his voice thick. "Healing you, I mean?"

Right. Because his hand was still hesitating there, just edging toward Kesst's bare arse. Toward where Skald had done all he'd done, leaving Kesst admittedly tender and sore, both inside and out.

"Of course I want you to keep going," Kesst confessed, into the safety of his arm. "But I'll warn you, I'll probably enjoy it, so..."

There was an odd little quiver in Eft's magic, surely about to finally pull away, to be finished with this—and then, unbelievably, a purposeful twitch of his hand downwards. Curving over Kesst's bare arse-cheek with a slow, deliberate gentleness, while his impossible magic spun and sparkled within.

Kesst's gasp was harsh, reflexive, deeply betraying—but oh, that only seemed to encourage it, the magic swirling with even more stunning, staggering purpose than before. That hand sliding up and down and sideways, caressing the inflamed skin, leaving it whole and prickling in his wake. Even slipping down to Kesst's thighs, now, nudging close between but not quite, and Kesst had to fight the urge to strain back, to part his legs, to know what that would *feel* like...

But then Eft moved up again, a little slower this time, more purposeful. Now easing carefully over Kesst's crease, while his magic kept delving closer, deeper. Finally focusing on where it felt the most tender, and also—gods damn it—on where it felt best. On where Skald had filled him with both agony and ecstasy, but this—

Another muffled groan escaped Kesst's choked throat, because this—this—was only ecstasy. Sheer, shouting, barrelling ecstasy, swallowing everything else in its strength. Eft's magic was *inside* him, Eft was damn near *fucking* him with it, and suddenly Kesst's craving was screeching, slavering, far too powerful to ignore.

"Would it be easier," he gasped, between thick breaths, "if you touched me inside?"

And oh, that had done it, Eft's magic and his touch once again shocked to raw, ringing stillness. Surely about to leave now, reject him now, surely—

But then, oh destroy Kesst where he lay, one of those fingers nudged him, just where he most wanted it. Where he was still slack and wet from Skald—from Skald's foul scent still *inside* him, gods curse it—but before Kesst could point that out, take it back, Eft's finger softly, gently pressed inside.

Kesst's moan was more of a shriek this time, his body pushing back into that touch—because damn it was good, it was more than good, it was quite possibly the most spectacular thing he'd ever felt in his *life*. Not even just the warm strength of that finger, sinking so easy and deep inside him, but the way the magic whirled and fluttered around it, again perhaps not even healing him now, but just making him feel it, wanting him to feel it too, oh, *oh*.

"More," Kesst gulped, before he could stop it, and yes, bless Eft, there was more. The magic swirling stronger, plucking and singing at every surrounding nerve, at every conscious thought. And Kesst only belatedly noticed that his cock had swollen rock-hard, straining and leaking into the fur beneath him, while his desperate arse clutched and milked and squeezed at that finger inside him. Needing it there forever, for always...

And then it *moved*. Circling a little against him, at the place where it already felt so damned good—and Kesst actually screeched this time, rocking back against it. "Fuck," he gasped. "*Fuck*, Eft."

And Eft might have laughed—laughed!—as his other hand skittered to brush against Kesst's arse, too. Not joining the other inside, no—but just stroking, caressing, adding more. Making Kesst flail and writhe against him, upon him, *more*— and if he abruptly scrabbled up onto his hands and knees, Eft certainly didn't seem to notice, or mind. Only shifting his hand a little more behind Kesst, so that he could meet him when he rocked back, sinking even deeper inside—and in return Kesst tossed his head as he howled, arching up, revelling in it, *glorying* in it.

"Oh," he moaned, as he plunged himself again and again onto that finger, into that touch, that sparkling, spectacular ecstasy. "Oh gods, oh Eft, make me, watch me, I—"

And yes, Eft was watching, their eyes finally meeting, holding, knowing. And it was at that perfect, impossible moment that Kesst's swollen, leaking cock locked, and then—let go. Surging out with torrent after torrent of hot, dizzying euphoria, painting the fur beneath him with rope after rope of thick scented seed, while Eft's magic kept sparking and soaring inside him. Until there was nothing else to spill, and Kesst's still-straining cock was squeezing out pathetic, painful little dribbles of white.

And then, finally, reality again. The slow, crushing, horrifying realization that Kesst had just railed himself onto a healer's single finger—and in the process, he'd no doubt forever tainted Eft with his scent, and with Skald's foul scent, too. And even worse, the way he'd done it, brazenly betraying himself as the needy, greedy waste that he was, *I'll do anything, please, whatever you want...*

He shot a furtive, chagrined glance at Eft, whose finger was still *inside* him, oh gods—and wait, whose finger was once again swirling out a delicious little shower of pleasure. Different than before, not nearly as intense, but more... playful?

Eft's cheeks and ears were looking distinctly flushed, his lips parted, his eyes dazed and glittering. And he held those eyes to Kesst's face as his finger slowly drew away, giving another one of those reassuring little sprays of warmth before it went.

"Well," Eft finally said, his voice very low, his tongue brushing his lips. "Thought you said you were a size queen, huh?"

The bastard. And in the giddy twisting relief, Kesst felt himself twitching, staring—and then, somehow, breaking into a gale of bright, merry laughter. A more genuine laugh than he'd perhaps given in years, his chest shuddering, his mouth grinning so hard it hurt.

"You—reckless—*menace*," he managed, between laughs, shaking his head. "How the *hell* did you do that?!"

Eft's face was still very flushed, and he glanced guiltily away, his hand rubbing at the back of his neck. "Well, instead of searching for what felt wrong, like I usually do," he replied, husky, "I went for what felt good."

Kesst laughed again, still shaking his head, and now smoothing his own trembling hands against his face and hair, almost as if he were some blushing innocent, gods damn it. "Please tell me you can do that with your cock," he heard his audacious voice whisper. "*Please*, Eft. I will worship at your feet for the rest of your too-short *life*."

Eft was laughing now too, and actually shrugging as his cheeks flushed even deeper. "Can't say I've ever tried," he replied, his voice a little shaky. "But I probably could, if I wanted to."

Kesst was staring again, marvelling again, the sudden surge of craving so strong he almost felt faint. "Unbelievable," he choked. "If this ever gets out, you realize you will have orcs lining up outside this dank little room for *years*. Throwing you all their gold, and *begging* you to plough them into the next moon."

And curse him, again, but even the thought of that—of Eft doing that with other orcs, rather than *him*—was bringing up the whispers of dread again, the misery, the shame. And suddenly Kesst was glancing down at the proof of that shame, the mess he'd so flagrantly made, the way his gluttonous, traitorous prick was *still* jutting straight out of him, long and ruddy and full.

"Hey," Eft murmured, much softer now, his hand brushing a shiver of heat up Kesst's arm. "So you'll keep this just between us, all right? You know I already have *more* than enough orcs coming down here and barking demands at me."

Oh. Kesst blinked back up at Eft's face, at that quiet earnest warmth in his eyes. At how they were now sliding up and down Kesst's bared body, studying, lingering, in a way that felt almost... reverent.

"And besides," he added, so soft. "You're the most beautiful of them all, you know. Gods, you should *see* yourself."

He gave a helpless-looking wave at Kesst's long loose hair, his hard torso, his still-straining, already-dribbling prick. As if this was truly something he liked, something he wanted, and it wasn't possible, not after today. It wasn't...

"I tell you, no taste whatsoever," Kesst finally heard himself say, his voice thick. "And no self-preservation. At *all*."

Eft laughed again, shaking his head—but Kesst was sure he saw something else in his eyes, this time. Something new... and something darker. An awareness, surely, of the very real danger they were courting in doing something like this, in risking Skald smelling this. They might get away with tonight—there'd at least been no seed exchanged, thank the gods—but if it went where Kesst so desperately wanted it to go? What if Eft had asked, and Kesst had just foolishly, mindlessly followed? What then?

But Eft's touch was here again, his hand gently sliding up Kesst's arm, swirling those flares of playful, comforting warmth in its wake. "Now don't you go off and start thinking again," he whispered. "Want you to sleep, Kesst. To do all your best healing for me, all right?"

All your best healing. It was exactly what Kesst had said to Skald, earlier that day—but Eft was taking it back, making it about him, about them. *For me.*

So Kesst nodded, watching, feeling oddly subdued, almost shy, as Eft tugged away the wet fur from underneath him, and reached to yank another one from a nearby bed. Smoothing it out beneath him before easing Kesst down onto it, his hand again stroking his back, spiralling out that warmth and comfort. That safety.

"Anything for you, Eft," Kesst heard himself whisper, as he drifted away into the darkness, into that beautiful, blissful safety. "Anything."

10

——————

I t felt like a long, long time before Kesst awoke again, blinking into the quiet warm darkness. Into an odd, floaty kind of peacefulness, curling around him, holding him close. Gods, he felt good, and he slowly stretched out on his fur, giving a huge, leisurely yawn, and—

And wait. *Wait.* Visions of the day before—the night before—were suddenly flooding through his thoughts, stomping down the peacefulness, and hurling out pure, palpable terror instead. What the hell. What in the gods' names had he *done*. Getting off with the healer? Risking Skald finding out about it? Blatantly bringing Eft's inevitable demise even closer than before?

And speak of the reckless devious menace, Eft was already turning around from Abjorn—one of several new unconscious orcs in the beds—and frowning toward Kesst. And then striding over, like he always did, his hand already reaching, about to touch Kesst's hair—

"No," Kesst gasped, flailing his arms, and lurching away in the bed. "No, Eft, damn it!"

Eft's big body had instantly frozen, his hand held in

midair—and curse it, but that was surely hurt in his eyes, in his audibly bobbing throat. But then he curtly nodded, and let his hand fall back to his side, and gave Kesst a brief, wan smile. And then turned and strode away, already reaching to spread his fingers back against Abjorn's head instead.

Something harsh and bitter plumed behind Kesst's ribs— gods, was he *jealous*?!—and he scrubbed at his face, huffed out a long, bracing breath. "We can't," he said to Eft's back, harder than he meant. "It's just too risky. Too dangerous."

Eft nodded, but didn't look back toward Kesst, either. And with the jealousy there was now a bleak, grating misery, clutching too tight in Kesst's gut. Gods, Eft had been so, *so* good to him. He'd given him so much pleasure last night. And now Kesst was returning all that with *this*?

Suddenly he couldn't bear being in this room any longer, he was going to end up rushing over there and begging—so he belatedly leapt out of bed, dragging his hands through his hair. "I need to go get some food and clothes," he snapped. "When's the last time you slept? Or ate a proper meal?"

Eft still didn't turn around, but Kesst could see his shoulder shrugging, could hear his slow exhale. "I honestly don't remember," he said. "A day or two ago, maybe?"

Good gods, this healer, and before Kesst could risk betraying anything else, he spun and stalked out of the room. First going back to the baths, spending far too much time trying to dilute Eft's scent as much as he possibly could, and then up to the otherwise empty little room where he some-times slept, and kept his few belongings. Skald had carelessly ruined the trousers he'd been wearing yesterday, and Kesst frowned as he pulled on his second best pair, and then painfully yanked a comb through his wet hair. But not braiding it back, because Skald preferred it down, and maybe—Kesst swallowed, his face foolishly heating—maybe Eft did, too.

He shoved that thought away as he next stalked down to

the kitchen, where some thoughtful Bautul hunter had thankfully left a deer carcass, still with some meat on its bones. So Kesst finished cleaning it, eating as he went, and then lit a fire to stew the bones over, preparing some broth for later use. And then he lightly braised the remaining meat, just enough to bring out the best flavour, before tossing it into a clean bowl, and stalking back down to the sickroom again.

"Here," he said to Eft, without preamble, as he strode over to where he was still working on Abjorn, and thrust the bowl into his chest. "Breakfast. *Morgunmatur.*"

Eft blinked at Kesst's face, and then down at the bowl—and then, to Kesst's distant, perverse satisfaction, his hands instantly abandoned Abjorn, and came up to cradle the bowl with palpable awe. "Really?" he said, sounding genuinely astonished. "For me?"

"Yes, for you," Kesst shot back. "If you really want to make your best attempt at surviving this ghastly mess, you need to at least take care of yourself. How the hell are you going to deal with all our constant rubbish if you're down here sleep-deprived and starving? So sit. Eat. *Borðaðu.*"

Eft kept blinking bemusedly at Kesst, but then he glanced down at the bowl, and that was surely hunger, flashing across his eyes and his scent. And he indeed dropped to sit on the end of Abjorn's bed, tossing a chunk of meat into his mouth, and exhaling a contented-looking sigh as he chewed.

"Gods, that's good," he said sheepishly. "Thanks. I've always been terrible at remembering to eat. To... *borðaðu?*"

Kesst was still standing before him, surely far too close— and he belatedly twitched backwards, and sat down facing Eft, on the foot of a still-unconscious Olarr's bed. "*Að borða,*" he corrected him. "To eat. I eat, *ég borða.* You eat, *þú borðar.*"

Eft's mouth was currently too full to speak, but he nodded, his mouth quirking up, his eyes warm and grateful. A look that was doing far too many things in Kesst's belly, and he looked away, crossing his arms over his chest.

"So how in the gods' names have you even *survived* all this time, then?" he asked, again more curtly than he meant. "If you're running around constantly provoking people, and forgetting to sleep and eat? Did you have an underling or something? Or maybe a besotted human mooning about after you?"

Eft swallowed his mouthful of meat, and gave another sheepish smile. "I did have a very generous family," he said. "My mother, and stepfather."

Wait. Kesst's brows had furrowed, his head tilting, following the implications of that. Eft *did have*, past tense. And a *stepfather*? But one who hadn't been able to teach him Aelakesh?

"Do you mean your stepfather was a *human*?" Kesst demanded. "Why? How? And what happened to him? And your mother?"

There was a brief twist on Eft's mouth, an unmistakable sadness in his scent. "Age, mostly," he replied. "My mother was older when my father, ah, *met* her. And after he died—in battle, I think—my stepfather came along. I'm quite sure the idea was to help my mother get rid of me, but thankfully they couldn't go through with it, so here I am."

He gave Kesst another self-deprecating smile as he bit off more meat, but Kesst was still frowning at him, and impatiently tapping his foot on the floor. "So you had no contact with orcs, all that time?" he snapped. "How in the gods' names did you learn to do all this healing, then?!"

Eft shrugged, gave yet another wry smile. "Uh, with humans?" he said. "And by the end, Grimarr had been coming around for a few years too. We lived near Bulmar—a little village in the south of Salven—but I didn't feel right about leaving, not until—"

That sadness was coiling through his scent again, his eyes dropped to his bowl. While Kesst just kept staring at him, his mouth agape, while his frantic brain sought to pull all this together. "So you've spent all these years swanning around out there healing *humans*, in the middle of a *war*?" he demanded. "How old are you again? And truly, how in the gods' names have you not gotten yourself *killed* yet?!"

Eft huffed a short laugh, though that was a telltale twitch of stubbornness now, on his scent and his eyes. "I'm thirty-two," he said. "And I tried to stay well out of the way, and out of the war. But people will overlook a hell of a lot—even an orc— when they or their loved ones are suffering, right? But, believe me"—he gave another brittle laugh, a furtive wave at his scarred face—"there have been a *lot* of killing attempts, too."

Good gods. So not only had Eft spent his life living with humans, healing humans, but he'd also almost been *killed* by them? Repeatedly? And *that* was where he'd gotten all these scars? Why he looked the way he did?

Kesst's stomach was churning and sinking again, his shoulders oddly hunching, his eyes glowering at Eft across from him. "Gods, you're so noble, it's fucking *painful*," he hissed. "How did you not have at least a few women—or men—throwing themselves at you, after you went and so gallantly saved their lives?"

Eft shrugged again, though that was another unmistakable twitch of stubbornness in his scent. "I wasn't interested," he said, not quite meeting Kesst's eyes. "Realizing now that my tastes don't really run to humans, you know?"

Oh. A bright, beautiful warmth was unspooling up Kesst's spine—Eft meant he liked orcs, he liked *him*—and suddenly, the memory of their disastrous first meeting was shifting, reorienting itself in his thoughts. *You are an orc*, Eft had said. *What, you want to look human?*

Kesst had to glance away again, biting at his lip, though he could feel Eft's eyes studying him. "How about you, then?" Eft's voice asked, quieter than before. "You speak with a human accent, too. Did you spend much time with your mother growing up? And were you able to use your magic?"

Kesst felt himself flinch, the bitter memories flaring behind his eyes, and he abruptly leapt to his feet, shaking his head. "I don't want to talk about it," he said, his voice again flat and curt. "Now, or ever."

Gods, he could still feel Eft's eyes on him, surely speculating, pitying him, and Kesst desperately shoved down that awareness as he stalked over to his bed, where he began intently smoothing out the fur. Waiting, waiting, until he could hear Eft shifting, clearing his throat.

"Right," he said. "Should get back to work, then. Thanks for the *morgunmatur*."

Kesst jerked a shrug, but didn't turn around, even as more of that miserable, too-familiar guilt studded through his chest. Why did he keep doing this, why did Eft keep returning it with such appalling kindness? Gods, it was painful, and Kesst shouldn't care, he should be leaving Eft alone for good, this was dangerous, deadly...

But unsurprisingly, he couldn't even seem to make himself leave the damned room again. Instead, he first spent an inordinate amount of time cleaning out the filthy fireplace, and then straightened out some of the other beds, too. And when the next injured, bloody orc staggered in—Ulfarr, a well-hung but highly belligerent Skai, who Kesst unfortunately knew far too well—he stalked over to intercept the situation, ignoring whatever bilge Ulfarr was spouting at Eft, and instead stepping between them, and fixing Ulfarr with a chilly, not-so-nice smile.

"You might as well just knock him out, Eft, and save us all the aggravation," Kesst loudly snapped, over Ulfarr's continued griping. "Now, unless you want to crack your thick head open on the floor, you can pick a bed, and lie down, and shut up. *Leggstu niður og þegiðu.*"

Ulfarr must have been in more pain than he wanted to admit, because he finally, grudgingly obliged, and soon was noisily snoring as Eft spread his fingers against his forehead. "Thanks, Kesst," he said, half-smiling over his shoulder. "*Leggstu niður og þegitu*, huh? Lie down and shut up? Seems like that one could come in handy."

"It's *þegiðu*, actually," Kesst said, with emphasis on the *ðu*. "But yes, it needs to become an essential part of your vocabulary. And therefore, I expect to hear it from you at *least* three more times today."

He belatedly twitched, and waited for Eft to stiffen at his presumptuousness, or maybe to finally tell him to get the hell out of his sickroom forever. Or even worse, to acknowledge the rising, unspoken truth that Kesst's scent was unmistakably present on Ulfarr, and Ulfarr's on him. And surely Eft could smell that, and gods, what must Eft think of him, and...

"I'll try," Eft replied, with another half-smile over his shoulder. "Are there any other crucial phrases I should know?"

Curse him, Kesst's *heart*, and he gave a sharp nod toward Eft's back. "Yes, actually," he said. "All things you should start telling me frequently. *Ég er svangur*, I'm hungry. *Ég er þreyttur*, I'm tired. *Ég þarf hjálp*, I need help. *Þú ert fallegur*, you're beautiful."

And what the hell was he doing, he was supposed to be keeping his distance, not trying to ingratiate himself into Eft's life, let alone fishing for juvenile compliments, damn it—but oh, that look of Eft's over his shoulder was why, that undeniable warmth, that relief, in his eyes.

"Good to know, thanks," he said, husky. "*Þú ert fallegur*, Kesst."

Kesst's grin stole across his face before he could stop it, along with a highly betraying flush to his cheeks. And he found himself tossing his hair over his shoulder, and even letting his tongue brush his lips. "I know," he said lightly. "But thank you. *Þakka þér fyrir.*"

Eft looked at him for a gratifyingly long moment, his eyes gone rather glazed. And far too late, Kesst forced himself to spin and stalk away, before he dug himself deeper, and made this mess even worse.

But clearly, self-destruction was too irresistible a temptation, because Kesst just couldn't seem to stay away from Eft as the day passed. Not only lurking around the cramped little room like he belonged there, but also giving Eft more words and phrases in Aelakesh, and plying him with more food and water, and continuing to make random improvements to the room, making it slightly less dank than before. And then even giving Eft all the gossip on the various sleeping orcs around them, explaining their clans, their preferences, their upbringings.

"So Olarr here keeps getting 'injured,' while out 'scouting,'" Kesst was currently saying, smirking down toward Olarr's huge unconscious body. "Never mind that he's a brilliant fighter, and that he always seems to come back doused with the exact same scent. Not suspicious at *all*, right?"

Eft was flashing an amused smile at Kesst, surely knowing—just as well as Kesst did—that the scent on Olarr was undoubtedly male, and undoubtedly human, too. "That explains a lot, actually," Eft said. "And what about this one?"

This one was Abjorn, his handsome grey face frowning in sleep, his black hair fanned out over the fur beneath him. "Ah, so Abjorn is probably the only Ka-esh around here who actually does any fighting," Kesst replied. "It's like he's forgotten that he's Ka-esh—well, apart from the collars and chains bit—and that he's supposed to be hunkered down here digging tunnels and mixing potions together. He spent way too much time growing up with my belligerent blood-brother Rathgarr, and Rath was completely obsessed with brawling, so as usual, I blame—"

And wait wait wait, Kesst was *not* talking about his family or his upbringing, ever—*especially* Rathgarr—but it was already too late. Eft's eyes widening, his head tilting, and was he going to ask, no no no—

Kesst had already flounced away again, stalking across the room, his shoulders hunched. Being a sulky brat, he knew, and surely Eft wasn't going to keep dealing with this tripe, he was going to smarten up and send Kesst away, and—

"Collars and chains, huh?" came Eft's mild voice behind him, and when Kesst whipped back around, frowning, Eft was wearing that wry smile again. "That would definitely explain some of these scars he's got. Is that a typical Ka-esh preference, then?"

Kesst had to stare for a moment, swallow down the lump in his throat—this *healer*—but he felt himself abruptly nodding, and then, without at all meaning to, drifting back toward Eft again. "Gods, yes," he replied. "I mean, not all of them, but it's definitely a *thing*. They even have a secret little pleasure-den a few corridors away from here, fully outfitted with all the whips and chains and paddles you could ever *dream* of. I thoroughly pity whatever poor schmuck ends up having to clean that place."

Eft's answering laugh was warm and tolerant, as if he'd truly already forgotten about Kesst's lapse, about Rathgarr. "And do *you* dream of that kind of thing, then?" he asked softly. "Chains, and the like?"

Kesst was staring at Eft again, because—first, he was asking, and had Kesst ever actually been asked about his own preferences before? And second, did Eft mean *he* wanted those things? And what kind of answer did he want on this, what if Kesst gave the wrong one, and—

"Do *you* want that?" Kesst heard his voice say, too high-pitched, almost panicked. "I mean, we've already established that I'm a greedy tart who'll do anything for cock, so I'm sure I—"

And gods, was he shuddering, because while Ofnir and Skald—and many others—had often been rough and careless with him, they'd rarely bothered with anything beyond their pricks and teeth and claws. And the thought of adding more, of being even more trapped than he already was, it was—

"Hey," Eft said, louder than before, and Kesst belatedly realized he'd abandoned Abjorn altogether, in favour of stepping closer, his hand reaching toward Kesst—but then abruptly dropping again, just in time. "Kesst. I wasn't looking for a specific answer, or even any answer at all, all right? Just wanting to know more about you, is all."

Oh. Kesst's breath was still coming in panting gulps, and Eft's smile was far too understanding, too kind. "And I told you, no putting down my best patient," he said. "He's making today better than any other day I've spent yet in this damned mountain, all right? He's clever, and funny, and thoughtful, and generous. Not to mention beautiful."

The lump in Kesst's throat was thickening again, and somehow he was easing closer, and attempting a wretched little smile. "*Fallegur*," he corrected Eft. "Or *stórglæsilegur*, if you want to get really excessive."

And Eft just kept smiling, with such ridiculous, impossible warmth in his eyes. "*Þú ert stórglæsilegur*, Kesst," he said, so soft. "And look, I'm the greedy one here, because I could look at you and smell you and listen to you all damned day, all right? Whether you like chains or not is completely irrelevant."

Kesst's swallow felt almost painful now, dragging against his constricted throat. "Well, I don't," he said thickly. "Like them, I mean. Just so you know."

Eft's smile didn't even slightly falter, and he nodded. "Was getting that impression," he murmured. "Luckily, I think I know a few other things you like."

The devious bastard, because Kesst's cock was already twitching to life in his trousers, and he couldn't even seem to make himself care if Eft tasted it, felt it. Or if he leaned a little closer into Eft, close enough that their hands brushed together—and oh, that was one of those playful flares of magic, rippling from Eft's fingers into his palm. Making him gasp, cracking something, breaking something—

And suddenly Kesst lurched forward, grasping for Eft's hand, yanking it against his bare waist. Feeling it tremble and skitter—the shakiness echoed in Eft's scent—before it shifted, deepened. Eft's fingers spreading, pressing, as his scent did the same, so strong and stubborn and singleminded it made the room spin. While Kesst grasped that hand tighter, pressed it closer, lower, *more*. He needed this, he needed Eft's sparkling shimmering warmth on his belly, down his trousers, around his swollen straining cock—

And Eft was, his fingers sliding smooth and easy around it, encircling it with his staggering, impossibly stunning touch. Driving a guttural, shameless moan from Kesst's mouth, his hips reflexively bucking forward, his hands suddenly, desperately clutching at Eft's tunic.

"Fuck," he gulped, broken, lost. "Oh, gods wreck me. Don't stop, Eft, don't you dare stop, you feel like—"

But at that precise perfect, horrible moment, Kesst smelled something. Something too strong, too close, something that stole away the pleasure and poured terror into its place—

And even as Kesst whirled away, he knew it was too late, too lost, everything destroyed, the end.

Skald was coming.

11

I f there was any hope left of salvaging this, of saving Eft for one more day, it was this.

"That hurts, you imbecile!" Kesst irritably barked, as Skald's huge, furious-tasting form lumbered into the room. "I asked you to heal it, not yank it off!"

He could feel Eft's sudden stiffness, an unmistakable shudder of rage as his eyes flicked toward Skald—but then, thank the gods, Eft yanked his hands back against his body, crossing his arms tightly over his tunic. "And *you* ought to know that healing isn't always painless," he hissed back. "If you really want your rubbish dealt with, you can bear a little discomfort in the process!"

It was the exact same tone he'd used on several obnoxious orcs these past days, and curse him, but Kesst felt himself flinch back a little, his head shaking. Eft didn't actually think all that, did he? He was just—just—

But Skald's huge deadly body just kept striding closer, his scent sickening in Kesst's nostrils—until he powerfully gripped Kesst's arm, roughly yanking him away from Eft. "You ought not to be down here, wench," he hissed at Kesst. "And this lying, craven bewitcher"—he shifted his heavy gaze to Eft—"ought to be on his knees for me, and begging for yet more of my mercy!"

Kesst could taste Eft's surging stubbornness, even as his narrowed eyes very briefly flicked down to the shining scimitar at Skald's side. And Kesst's fear was swelling, screeching, because despite Eft's promises to try, there was still no way he would ever kneel for Skald, ever—

"Forgive me, sir," said Eft's wooden voice, as he brought his fist to his chest, his head lowered, the way Grimarr had taught him. "I've just been focused on healing these injured orcs, and thus serving your captain and your mountain, as I've sworn to do."

Skald's eyes glanced darkly around the room, clearly taking in the assortment of unconscious orcs still in the beds. Drafli, Olarr, Abjorn, Silfast, Ulfarr. And for the first time, it distantly occurred to Kesst that—with the glaring exception of Ulfarr—these were all orcs who were likely to be loyal to Grimarr. And not only that, but their fighting skills ranged from good to spectacular. As if his most calculating brother had stuck them all down here... on purpose?

"Ach, *healing*," hissed Skald now, with a mocking bark of a laugh. "And this is why your fresh scent is all over *my* wench's prick, whilst he yet stands here healthy and hale before me!"

It took all Kesst's wherewithal to keep himself still, but Eft didn't look even slightly alarmed, that stubbornness still thick in his scent. "Yes, Kesst still stands, thanks to me," he said flatly. "But he is *not* fully healed yet, no matter how he looks. He still has two broken ribs, his chest wall is still healing, and his blood pressure and circulation are still erratic, and therefore in need of constant monitoring. Not to mention all the new contusions and lacerations he's recently gained! And without me managing his pain, he would certainly *not* be still standing here, and complaining at me!"

He didn't look at Kesst as he'd spoken this time, but Kesst still felt himself twitch at those words, at the certain truth behind them. Eft had really been doing all that for him, all this time? He was still managing his pain, even now?

But Skald clearly wasn't swayed, the taste of his terrifying anger surging higher in the air around him. "You *dare* speak to me thus, bewitcher?" he growled. "I said, you are to kneel, and—"

And finally, finally, Kesst lurched into motion, flailing toward Skald, his smile pasted to his face. "Skald, dearest," he said, his voice unnaturally high-pitched, his hands sliding up Skald's bare chest. "Your concern for me is very much appreciated, but I *did* ask this blockhead to fix me. As he said, my— ahem—*circulation* was clearly still not quite... functioning, in quite a crucial area. And I couldn't bear the thought of not performing properly for you, so—"

But it wasn't working, Skald was still glowering at Eft, his rage still seething, his big hand dropping to grip his sword-hilt. "This bewitcher yet ought to know," he hissed, "not to touch what belongs to me, without my leave! Mayhap now I shall command him to put all your wounds back again, wench, one by one! Or mayhap make him watch as I do so? That shall teach him, I ken?"

Kesst had frozen stiff against Skald, the horrifying dread curling up his spine, and he couldn't stop the gulp from escaping his throat. "No, Skald," he gasped. "No, let's not, I am so finished with him anyway. Why don't we just go, I'll give you a nice deep suck, make you something tasty for supper, and—"

But Skald had roughly shoved Kesst aside, and drew out his scimitar with a fluid, deadly flourish. "Or mayhap," he purred, "we watch whilst the bewitcher bleeds out onto this floor. This shall be even better, ach?"

He was already advancing toward Eft, no, no, *no*, and Eft was backing away from him, his hands raised, his unease finally swirling above his fierce stubborn rage. "Killing me will not help you," he said, his voice still astonishingly steady. "What happens when you need healing next? Or your captain? Is it not your calling to protect him at all costs, so that—"

But no, no, it was the worst, *worst* thing to say, Skald's fury flashing cold and sickening in Kesst's gut. "*Blasphemy*," he growled. "My captain shall never need healing, with me at his side! And thus, he shall never have need for the likes of *you*!"

With that, he lunged forward, his scimitar sweeping in a shining, deadly arc toward Eft's body. And Kesst was shouting, lunging, terror flying and screaming, no, no, NO—

But it was too late, too late. And Skald's blade swept straight across Eft's chest, gouging a thick red line in its wake—

Eft's scent shot through with shock, with unspeakable agony, his eyes flashed wide—and then he stumbled back, crashed to the floor, and went still.

12

————

For a long, horrifying instant, Kesst just stood there, and stared at Eft on the floor. At how the blood was already welling through his sliced-open tunic, how his body was erratically twitching, his mouth contorting, his eyes staring blankly at the ceiling, while pure agony poured through his scent.

And was it fatal, was he dying, and Kesst wanted to scream, to vomit, to weep. Skald couldn't do this, he couldn't, he was walking toward Eft with his sword out, he was going to finish it, no, no, *no*—

And somehow Kesst had rushed between them, his shaking hands clutching to Skald's huge arms. And without thinking, without hesitating, he drew up the magic. Dragged it up from the very depths of his being, yanking it out in gulp after desperate gulp, until it surged and churned, pitching for escape—and then he let it pour out his mouth.

"And when the powerful warrior killed the healer," he heard himself croak, his voice no longer his own, "after the healer had so faithfully saved his wounded lover's life, the gods were sore dismayed. And in their wisdom and justice, upon the warrior they visited many wounds that could not be healed. Wounds that brought pain, and weakness, and *shame*."

Skald had thankfully, briefly gone still, his eyes blinking unseeing at Kesst's face. And Kesst drew up more of the magic, poured it into terror and ice, fuelled it into his breath and his eyes...

"Boils that oozed and festered," he continued, his voice deepening, his hands rising between them. "Spasms that weakened his hands and feet. Darkness that clouded his sight. He could no longer walk, speak, or wield his sword, and instead writhed alone in torment and in grief. And in his weakness, he was of no further good to his captain, his clan, and his kin— and thus they left him to rot in disgrace, until he was forever forgotten!"

His voice had gone hard and vicious by the end, ringing with its strange, chilling command throughout the room. And Skald was staring now, caught, for this moment at least, and Kesst gulped for more air, more strength. "But in another life, the warrior saw the folly in such a killing," he continued, "and let the healer be. He walked away, whole and hale, and lived for yet another day. And he kept living, as long as he kept the healer from his mind, and kept his distance from the healer's domain!"

The words echoed and hung, and Kesst's eyes and his hovering hands and his held breath kept them there, dangling, sinking, settling. Embedding themselves into Skald's blank eyes, into his thoughts, into his memories...

"Get out," Kesst hissed. "Now."

And he waited, waited, his eyes burning on Skald's, his heart thundering through his chest. Until finally, *finally*, Skald spun and lumbered out, his hand rubbing powerfully at his eyes, his sword still dripping Eft's fresh blood onto the stone floor.

Kesst stood there, rigid and vehement, until Skald had gone

out of sight—and then felt himself swaying, the strength pooling away in a rush. Leaving him hollow and shaky all over, his ears ringing, his breaths coming in desperate gasps through his throat. Eft. *Eft.*

He spun so fast he nearly fell, staggering across the room. To where Eft was still lying sprawled on his back, a small black pool growing beneath him, his tunic now soaked with red blood, his eyes unseeing on the ceiling, his scent still reeking with pain...

"Eft!" Kesst choked, dropping to kneel in the warm sticky blood, as his hands frantically hovered over the deadly wound slicing open Eft's chest. "Oh gods, please say you're still alive, what can I do, what can I *do*—"

He was desperately searching Eft's pale, sweaty face, his distant, dazed-looking eyes. And suddenly there was the wildest urge to start screaming, to rage and wail and beg, he'd just risked *everything* for this, and now Eft was dying, he was dead, he was—

When abruptly, Eft's chest rose. Rose, inhaling, breathing— and Kesst nearly laughed, or sobbed, with his screeching giddy relief. And Eft's hazy eyes were even meeting his, holding, saying, *look at me, listen.*

"Need this—bound," Eft rasped, his voice very thin. "Cloth."

Bound, with cloth. And curse it, there was no cloth here beyond their clothes, and the bedding was all furs—so in a flailing twist of motion, Kesst kicked off his own trousers, and carefully spread them over Eft's chest. But then realized that he had to get them under him to tie them and apply any pressure, and Eft was far too big for him to lift alone, and oh gods oh gods—

"Help—sit up," Eft croaked now, his glazed eyes darting up toward the stone wall behind him. "Then bind."

Oh. Kesst was fervently nodding, even as he hovered uncertainly, not knowing how the hell to manage this—but then Eft raised his arms, as he pulled up his knees. And Kesst instinctively leaned in, grasping him carefully beneath the arms, while Eft gripped a bloody hand at Kesst's shoulder, and pushed back with his feet. Giving a broken-sounding grunt as he scrabbled backwards, the pain in his scent flashing even higher—but then he was indeed propped up against the wall, his legs outstretched before him, his head tilted back, his teeth gritted with visible agony.

But it was enough, enough for Kesst to first ease the trousers around Eft's torso, and then bind them as tightly as he could. And Eft was nodding as he exhaled, his arm now come to rest over the binding, his fingers spreading wide.

Because... wait. Wait. He was... *healing* himself.

Oh gods, Eft was healing himself, the beautiful wonderful bastard—and Kesst felt a sudden, hoarse sob escape his throat as he knelt there and watched, marvelled, and silently pleaded with every god he'd ever known.

"Don't you dare stop, Eft," he croaked. "You keep going. Keep breathing. We need you. *I* need you, damn it."

Eft was holding Kesst's eyes, he was listening, and that might have even been a nod. And now his other hand had come to join the first against his heaving chest, while a harsh exhale shuddered from his throat.

"Good," Kesst whispered. "Good. You keep doing that, love. You find everything that's wrong, and fix it. Don't stop."

Eft's gaze had oddly flared at that highly betraying word *love*, but he gave another unmistakable nod, his tongue brushing his dry-looking lips. And wait, he'd lost so much blood, surely he needed water, if nothing else—so Kesst leapt up, rushed away to grasp a waterskin, and rushed back. And when he saw Eft nod again at the sight of it, he yanked out the cork, and raised it to Eft's mouth.

Eft willingly drank, though his swallows looked distinctly

painful. And when he was clearly done, slightly turning his head, Kesst carefully wiped at his mouth, and attempted a miserable-feeling little smile. "Anything else I can do," he breathed, "you just tell me, Eft. Anything."

Eft's chest rose and fell, something shifting in his dazed eyes on Kesst's. "Keep—talking?" he whispered, so weakly Kesst almost couldn't hear it. "Distracts—from the pain. Makes it—easier."

Kesst was already nodding, scooting to kneel a little closer beside Eft's sprawled legs. "Of course I will," he said firmly, though his thoughts were spiralling again, because what the hell did Eft want him to say, everything in his head was Skald and misery and death, surely Eft didn't need to hear that, and...

"Tell me... how?" Eft's thin voice broke in, his eyes purposefully angling toward the door, toward where Skald had gone. "What you..."

Kesst couldn't help a wince, and wait, Eft had caught that, and now he was wincing, too. "Or—not," he rasped. "Whatever you—"

And gods, Eft was *not* feeling guilty about asking, trying to make *Kesst* feel better, not in a state like this—and Kesst flapped his hands toward him, shaking his head. "Of course I'll tell you," he croaked back. "I just—you might not like it, you know?"

Eft actually twitched a shoulder, as if he were shrugging, and Kesst had to choke back a sudden, reflexive noise, perhaps a sob. And he was nodding again, and somehow feeling his hand come to Eft's shoulder, gently gripping against it, drinking up his stubborn strength, even now.

"It's... more of the old magic," he whispered. "Obviously. Our fathers called it galdr-telling. Sometimes galdr-spinning. Telling tales."

Eft gave another one of those almost-nods, his eyes still fixed to Kesst's—and Kesst drew in air, squared his shoulders.

"There's always power in tales, right?" he continued, with a hoarse little laugh. "Well, this—whatever the hell this is—just makes whatever tale you're telling that much stronger. More real."

Eft's eyes were shifting again, looking dazed again, or maybe even awed. "And you can," he began, "use it to…"

"To suggest?" Kesst finished, with another sharp little laugh. "To manipulate? To make them forget? Yes. Indeed. But"—he drew in more air—"it's not infallible. It doesn't always work. And the listener's awareness always returns, but it's just a matter of when, and how much they remember. If I don't put too much into it, it's usually only a moment or two—but the more I push, and the stronger the connection between me and my listener, the longer it lasts."

Eft's brow had furrowed, his gaze angling toward the door again—and he didn't need to ask this time, because Kesst nodded, and laughed yet again. "I pushed that tale harder than I've pushed anything in my life," he whispered. "I probably got us a few days' reprieve. But after that, if Skald finds us here when he comes back"—he dragged in a shaky breath—"we're *dead*, Eft. You and me both. You should have *seen* what Kaugir did to the last orc who could compel him like that."

Eft's brows were still furrowed, still wanting more, and again it was easy enough to follow. "And no, the rest of them don't know," Kesst continued. "Not really. They know I tell good tales, so when they want one, I give them one. It's just another entertaining trick from the court jester, right? All part of the amusement package, together with a deep throat, a tight hole, and a pretty face."

His voice had gone low and bitter, his eyes not quite meeting Eft's anymore. But his hand was still on Eft's shoulder, surely clinging too tight—and that was the feel of Eft's shoulder again twitching, just a little. And when Kesst risked a look at Eft's eyes, they were giving him that familiar stubborn frown, his bottom lip jutting out, his sentiment far too clear. *No putting down my best patient*, he might as well have said.

Another high-pitched sound escaped Kesst's throat, but he had to keep talking, keep distracting. Anything Eft wanted to know, anything he'd ever asked...

"Before my mother died," Kesst heard his wavering voice continue, "I used to spend half my days telling her tales. To help her forget. She was mated to my father, you see, but by then he was completely destroyed by all the war and fighting, and barely knew our names anymore. And my mother was very beautiful, with a lovely scent, and Kaugir wanted her, wanted another son, and so—"

He couldn't finish, suddenly, his vision flooding with the memories, with his blank-eyed father, his weeping mother with her belly rounded yet again. With his big, powerful brother Rathgarr loud and vicious and reckless, consumed by fighting, by drink and raucous laughter... and in between, by ever longer spells of strange, stilted silence.

"It's why I have this human accent," Kesst made himself continue, keep talking, keep talking, "and not my father's. I didn't want to sound like an orc, I wanted to sound like *her*. To be something safe for her. To remind her of her home."

Eft's eyes hadn't once left Kesst's as he'd spoken, listening, acknowledging, knowing. "Your mother must have," Eft whispered, hoarse, "loved you. So much."

Kesst couldn't deny his sob this time, his erratic little shrug, because yes, she'd so often told him she loved him, but at the same time, he'd never been able to save her, either. And instead, he'd learned to do exactly what she'd done, to smile and wheedle, to placate and lie. To pretend at desire, to find her pleasure where she could, to only weep when she was alone. To do whatever it took to survive.

But she still hadn't survived, and neither had any of her other sons after Rathgarr and Kesst, because this mountain—

Kesst's own clan, his own kind—had still caught up with her in the end. All that effort, all that hiding and lying, and all it had done was gain her a few more years of helpless, hopeless misery, trapped in a prison, serving the vile orcs she'd both desired and hated.

"And then she died," Kesst choked, his voice cracking. "And my father barely even noticed. And Rath, he swore to me we'd find a way out of here, he *promised* he'd keep me safe. But then he—he just *left*. Disappeared. His scent gone off due north, alone. And he didn't even—didn't even say—"

Kesst couldn't keep going, because something dark and dangerous was knocking against his ribs, his head shaking, the grief threatening to explode from his throat. Too much to bear, to face, he couldn't, he couldn't, he—

"Hey," croaked Eft's voice, snapping Kesst's gaze back to his pale, sweaty face. But that was surely concern in his eyes—*concern!*—and he'd even lifted a bloody hand from his own chest, his fingers skittering against Kesst's forearm. Flaring him a tiny flicker of that magic, so much weaker than usual, and Kesst suddenly twitched back to awareness again, and belatedly glowered down at Eft's watching eyes.

"You do *not* stop healing yourself for my rubbish, you reckless menace," he hissed, and without at all meaning to, he'd shifted up to carefully straddle his body over Eft's thighs, so he could better meet his hazy eyes. "No. And no more sob stories, either. You focus on healing. On fixing this. That's *all.*"

An unmistakable warmth had crept across Eft's eyes, his breath slowly exhaling as he nodded. And to Kesst's twitching surprise, he lifted his knee up behind Kesst's still-straddling body—which was, incidentally, fully bared—almost as if to hold him there. As if he liked him there. Wanted him to stay.

"Then—tell me one?" he whispered at Kesst, his voice just slightly steadier than before, the pain perhaps softer in his scent. "A tale?"

Oh. Yes, yes, of course Kesst would do that, and he fervently nodded, and settled himself a little closer. Ignoring the sensation of Eft's bloody trousers brushing against his bollocks, and attempting a smile as he drew in breath.

"Long ago, in a land across the sea," he began, "there was once a lost, lonely mortal. He was kept prisoner by his cruel masters, and he had abandoned all hope of freedom."

He hadn't pushed the magic this time, just letting it curl out around the words as it wished—but Eft's watching eyes were already looking rather more dazed than before. So as a precaution, Kesst dropped a hand to spread against Eft's arm on his bloody chest, where he could taste his magic still working deep inside, thank the gods.

"But in the heavens," Kesst continued, "the gods finally saw the mortal's plight, and heard his pleas. And in their benevolence, they sent an angel to meet him. To shine a light in his darkness."

Eft's eyes were still watching, his magic still working, so Kesst kept speaking, attempting another smile toward Eft's face. "But upon their first meeting," he murmured, "the mortal greatly feared the angel, and his light. It showed how the darkness was not only all around him, but it had crept inside him. It tainted and corrupted him. It made him weak and afraid."

And perhaps Eft wasn't quite as caught in the tale as Kesst had thought, because his bottom lip was jutting out again, that familiar stubbornness skidding into his scent—and Kesst huffed a laugh as he shook his head, and took the liberty of brushing his thumb against that pouting mouth.

"But the angel was not so easily defeated," he murmured, as he let his thumb linger, feeling the warmth of Eft's breath, the surprising softness of his lips. "He faced the mortal with his iron will, and his great power, and his unspeakable pleasures. Gaining the mortal's trust, and drawing him ever closer, until..."

Eft's unblinking eyes were decidedly rapt now, his magic stuttering as it actually flooded stronger, and as the pain in his scent faded further still. As if Kesst's silly little tale truly was helping him, distracting him, and suddenly there was nothing more crucial than keeping Eft's eyes on him like this, tasting that magic pouring, working, *saving.*

"Until the mortal was wholly enthralled," he breathed, "and longed to spend all his days on his knees, deep in worship at the angel's feet. And he dreamt of the day the angel would grant him leave to taste all the fullness of his sweet bounty, and to drink until he was fat and content."

His thumb was still brushing Eft's lips, his fingers now slightly stroking at Eft's scarred cheek. Feeling how Eft's unsteady breath exhaled against his palm, how the warmth seemed to deepen beneath his touch. How the pain had faded a little further still, lost in this, in *him.*

"And then what?" Eft whispered, into Kesst's thumb. "What happened next?"

Kesst felt his smile pulling at his mouth, so slow, so affectionate, so *relieved.* "You tell me, love," he murmured back. "Would the angel grant his worshipper such a gift? Allow him to kneel, and drink as he pleases?"

And oh, Eft was nodding. Saying yes. His eyes still rapt on Kesst's face, his tongue briefly brushing against Kesst's still-stroking touch.

"Hell, yes," he breathed. "Yes, Kesst. Drink me."

13

rink me.

A furious shiver shot up Kesst's spine, choking a gasp from his throat. Eft wanted that. Wanted *him*.

But once again, Eft's breath shuddered and exhaled, his dazed eyes refocusing on Kesst's face. "But only," he whispered, "if you really want it. If you—"

But Kesst was sliding his whole hand up to cover Eft's mouth, now, his own mouth pulling into a tenuous little smile. "Of course I want it," he whispered back. "Want anything you'll give me, love. Just as long as you keep on healing like that."

Eft's eyes shifted, settled, his breath again exhaling, his magic shuddering out even stronger than before. And with it, Kesst could also feel an unmistakable swelling beneath Eft's trousers, jutting up between his own parted legs. Hard for him. Wanting him. Wanting Kesst to taste him.

Kesst drew in a shaky breath—gods, was he *nervous?*—and slowly, carefully, dropped his trembling hands down to Eft's waist. Just brushing over his bloody tunic, while watching for any hint of new pain in Eft's eyes—but they only kept blinking back toward him, focused, intent, almost reverent.

So Kesst shifted himself further downwards, let his fingers spread wider, lower, toward Eft's trousers. Skittering a little as they nudged against that hardness, felt it nudge back up against him. Felt how it was—it was—

Wait. What? The *hell*?

Kesst twitched and stilled all over, his eyes dropping to the bulge beneath his hand, while another furious flaring shiver chased up his spine. Because gods, this... this couldn't be it. This couldn't be real. Eft could not be the most well-hung orc he'd ever met in his life, this was *not happening*...

He shot an accusing look up at Eft's face, at where Eft was now looking almost *amused*, damn the devious bastard. And suddenly Kesst needed to see this, to disprove this, there was no way, *none*, and his hands were desperately pulling at the trousers' waist, yanking them downwards, and...

Well, fuck. *Fuck*. Because there, lying with breathtaking casualness against Eft's belly, was quite possibly the most perfect, most magnificent prick Kesst had ever seen in his life. It was shockingly long, surpassing even Simon's—but unlike Simon's, it was slimmer and smoother, jutting out straight and strong from the soft nest of black curls at its base, until it tapered into an elegant, already-slick grey tip. Gods, it would feel so good, it would be such a joy to ride, it would ease so smoothly into you, and then sweetly, stubbornly annihilate you.

And most devastating of all, there wasn't a single damned scent upon it. It had never, *ever* been touched before, by another orc or a human. And Kesst was about to taste it? To cover this impossible marvel with his scent, and his *alone*?!

Kesst truly could not move, and he only distantly noticed that his mouth had fallen open, and a desperate, guttural moan had escaped from his throat. At least, until Eft—the wounded devious *cheat*—huffed a sound that might have been a laugh. *Laughing* at Kesst, over this, and Kesst's eyes darting upwards found Eft indeed still looking amused, and maybe a little sheepish, too.

"You did *not*," Kesst managed, through his tangled tongue, "tell me about this!"

His voice sounded quite frankly accusing, enough that he gave a belated wince—but Eft was actually shrugging, and twitching a shy little smile toward him. "Didn't want to get my hopes up," he replied, husky and low. "And wanted you to like *me*."

To like him, and not just his cock. As if *not liking Eft* was something Kesst would ever have been able to accomplish, ever, and here was the stunning realization that he liked Eft more than he'd ever liked anyone else in his life, excepting his mother. And now that person—*this* person—was walking around with *this* down his trousers?!

"You devious deceitful *menace*," Kesst croaked, shaking his head. "Of course I'd still like you, no matter what you had down here. But this"—his eyes dropped again, drinking up the sight with blatant, breathless reverence—"this is *such* a brilliant bonus, Eft. Good gods above, it's exactly what I like. More than Skald's. More than Grim's. More than *Simon's*."

If Eft cared about being compared to the previous orcs Kesst had most enjoyed, he certainly didn't show it. And instead, that beauty at his groin bobbed a little upward, as if to say, *Yes. Good. Look at me. Touch me.*

Gods destroy him, there was no possible way Kesst could resist that command, that *offering*—and he swallowed hard as he gently, carefully stroked a finger against it. Feeling it flex back against his touch, swelling even fuller, the skin at its head peeling fully down, showing off that tapered, glossy crown. And oh it was perfect, it was so gorgeous it hurt, and it needed more than touching, damn it, it needed to be lavished, adored, covered in Kesst's scent and his worship—

And before he'd quite realized it, Kesst had scrabbled

further downwards, kneeling between Eft's sprawled thighs. Bending close over him, inhaling that prick's delectable scent deep—and then gently, so gently, he settled his tongue to its base, and slowly, sweetly licked up.

It bobbed hard against Kesst's tongue, in tandem with Eft's satisfyingly deep groan—and Kesst again slid a hand up to Eft's arm, making sure his magic was still working, still healing. And then flashing him a brief, approving smile, before ducking his head, and licking up again.

He'd used a little more pressure this time, revelling in the taste of that silken untouched skin beneath his tongue, in the way it shuddered even fuller and longer than before. Already sputtering out a bead of rich seed at the tip, like the beautifully obliging marvel it was, and Kesst was already there, catching that seed upon his tongue, groaning as the taste of it swarmed across his mouth. Oh, it tasted so good, tasted just like Eft, like his glorious magic made into mead, just for him, only for him...

Eft had moaned again too, the sound broken and harsh, and Kesst's glance up at his face found his eyes wide, shocked, unblinking. But surely awed, too, or maybe even eager, the taste of his pain almost entirely faded now—so Kesst made a show of brazenly licking his lips, making that dazzling scent his, his, *forever*.

"Fuck, you taste good," he murmured. "So good, love. Give me more?"

Eft groaned again, but oh, that perfect cock was already squeezing out more, giving Kesst exactly what he wanted. And Kesst slipped his fingers into those dark curls, circling around Eft's base, holding that shocking length straight up toward his mouth. So Eft could watch him tasting it, could watch it ooze out sweet and thick upon his tongue.

"So good," Kesst purred, between licks, as he let his hungry tongue learn that smooth head, let it stroke and flick and linger. Let himself smear the sweetness up and down and around, making the scent stronger and deeper, swarming the air with its richness. While his other hand belatedly dropped lower, between Eft's thighs, finding—his eyes fluttered, hard—a pair of huge bulging bollocks, swollen full of seed, nearly too big to fit in his fingers.

"You—damned—*menace*," Kesst gulped, as he frantically caressed them, rolled them between his fingers. "Don't tell me you have huge loads, too. *Don't*."

But his eyes were surely pleading on Eft's, his tongue still desperately licking, and Eft was still staring, still with that same awestruck wonder in his eyes and his scent. "I won't," he whispered, the utter bastard—and Kesst's moan was more like a cry this time, his eyes squeezing shut. And suddenly he needed to know, needed to taste it, so urgently it was drowning everything else, please please please—

He set upon that cock with sudden, furious abandon, sucking it down, sinking it hard and deep into his throat. Only vaguely noticing how Eft shuddered and seized beneath him, because oh, he was in Kesst's mouth, he was in his *throat*, and Kesst could distantly taste his magic still working, still healing himself, even stronger than before. And Kesst could have sobbed at the feel of it, the truth of it, he'd barely even taken him halfway, gods *damn*—

So he sucked deeper, harder, pouring into this everything he'd ever learned, everything he could possibly muster. Swirling his tongue, deepening the suction, convulsing his greedy throat around that hard delving head, taking it as deep as he possibly could. And also cradling and caressing those bollocks with one hand, while the other one began seeking, stroking, exploring. First Eft's taut lower belly, then the hard line of his hipbone, then his big, softly furred thighs. And when those thighs trembled beneath Kesst's touch, and perhaps even slightly parted, Kesst dared to delve his fingers lower, deeper between. To where many orcs wouldn't tolerate being touched, most of all by a weak pretty wench like him...

But oh, Eft's moan had only darkened, his knees spreading purposefully wider. And Kesst made a harsh, strangled sound around the cock in his mouth as he stroked and caressed and learned, as he found Eft's soft puckered heat, felt it eagerly kissing back against him, fuck, *fuck*—

He moaned again, sucking, seeking, driving Eft's hardness deeper into his spasming throat, while the tip of his finger gently nudged into that dark silken clutch. And the way Eft groaned and grasped at him, oh this was destroying him, it was ripping him open, flaying him alive, too much, too much...

His own seed surged up without warning, spewing out from his engorged cock with wild erratic desperation. Flashing Kesst with pulse after pulse of hard convulsing ecstasy, crushing him, consuming him, stealing away his scent his sight his heart—

And suddenly there was even more, more, because Eft was blowing out, too. Pouring down Kesst's throat in a sharp furious blast of rich swarming heat, so strong and so thoroughly over-whelming that Kesst actually *choked* on it. His throat frantically, helplessly convulsing as that succulent, still-pouring nectar filled his mouth, spilled out his lips, pooled thick and messy down his chin...

But there was still more, still so much, and fuck, he was *wasting* it—and finally Kesst managed to recover enough to swallow again, to keep taking it down his throat. Not using any finesse now, just desperately sucking and slurping on that spraying head, like he'd never done this before in his life. Like their places had been reversed, and *he* had somehow become the blushing, untouched innocent.

But once the flow had finally slowed, and Kesst had sucked out the last few drops and raised his head, Eft didn't look inno-cent at all. In fact, he looked downright ravenous. Vicious. *Victorious.* His eyes blazing with hunger, his face flushed, his sprawled body painted with blood and—oh. With copious spurts of Kesst's fresh seed. But Eft hadn't even seemed to notice, and instead he was licking his lips, his tongue long and lingering as his eyes dropped to Kesst's mouth.

He didn't even need to say it, because Kesst's shuddering, tingling body was already pushing up, closer—and then he slowly, carefully leaned in, and pressed his mouth to Eft's. Their lips just brushing at first, so soft, so tentative—but oh, Eft's kiss back was hard, sloppy, eager. His tongue swirling and seeking, tasting himself on Kesst, and Kesst couldn't help his harsh, answering groan into Eft's mouth, the greedy press of his body against him. As if saying, *Yes, lick me, like me, drink me up, please, please...*

And Eft was still obliging, artless and shameless, his slick tongue now dragging against the mess on Kesst's chin, his cheeks, his jaw. While Kesst just kept leaning into it, shuddering, feeling his shaky hand spread against Eft's shoulder, against something slippery, against—

Right. His own abundant mess, proof of how he'd once again blown—with impressive spread and distance—without even being touched. And Eft had stilled, following that, his gaze angling toward Kesst's hand, the hunger again flashing through his eyes...

"Taste you, too?" Eft breathed, his tongue again brushing his lips. "Please?"

Oh. Oh. Kesst swallowed hard as he nodded, swiping his shaky finger into more of his own dripping mess, and bringing it to Eft's waiting mouth. Watching as Eft sucked that finger with firm, fervent purpose, his eyes still blazing on Kesst's—and then his beautiful magic suddenly studded into Kesst's finger, swarming his entire hand with shivering, sparkling ecstasy.

Kesst moaned at the same time Eft did, their eyes still

locked together, their bodies trembling beneath the strength of it. And it almost hurt to draw that finger away, to find more of his own seed on Eft's skin, to slip it back between Eft's lips—but oh, his reward was even more spectacular, more thought-shattering than before. Magic sparking and dancing, flooding him with warmth and affection and safety. Eft wanted this. Wanted him. Wanted to taste him. Wanted his scent on his *mouth*.

So Kesst kept going, kept feeding Eft his spent seed, lost in the dazed spinning wonder, in the unthinkable unreality of this moment. Until his hand, seeking a little lower, somehow came back with something red on it. With... with Eft's blood.

"Wait," Kesst croaked, his head shaking, while his blunted, distant thoughts suddenly roared to life again. "Wait. You are not—*not*—supposed to be—"

His other hand had belatedly gripped back to Eft's arm, still feeling that magic working, healing—but it was damned well supposed to be stronger, Eft was supposed to be focusing on that, not this. And Eft, the stubborn bastard, was actually pouting back at Kesst, and dismissing his deadly, bloody wound with a curt, irritable wave of his hand.

"You're more important," he whispered, his eyes still shifting, shining, ravenous. "More."

It took all Kesst's willpower to lean a little backward, attempt a shake of his head. "No, you raging *menace*," he whispered back. "You do not give me one more twitch of your magic until this is fixed. Not *one*."

Eft looked fully ready to argue, his brows heavily furrowed, his mouth opening—but then he grimaced, his eyes squeezing shut, his head tilting a little back against the wall. "Right," he rasped. "Sorry."

Gods, he could not be apologizing for that, and suddenly Kesst had to touch him again, find his face again, draw Eft's hazy gaze back toward him. "You know I want it," he breathed.

"So much. But I want you more. I need you, Eft. You have no idea how much I—how I—"

He couldn't finish, shaking his head, and oh, Eft was smiling, smiling at Kesst with those dazed, shining eyes. "Yeah," he whispered back. "Forgot to even try the magic when you were sucking me. Gods, Kesst, nothing has ever felt so good in my *life*."

Kesst barked a hoarse laugh, smoothing a shaky hand against his hair. "Agreed," he replied, breathless. "Enough that *I* could barely take you halfway, and apparently forgot how to swallow. *Me*! I'll have you know, Eft, I am usually *very* good at this."

Eft was still smiling, so reverent, so affectionate. "It was perfect," he whispered. "Gods, you're perfect. Beautiful. *Fallegur. Stórglæsilegur.*"

An undeniable heat was swarming Kesst's cheeks, and he felt himself giving a slow, shy-feeling smile back, even as he tossed his hair over his shoulder. "You just wait," he replied, "until you fully heal this mess, and I suck your gorgeous prick properly. I will have you *screaming* for me, love, while I bury you all the way down my throat. And in return, you'll pour out *all* of that delicious load, straight into my hungry belly. Right where it damn well belongs."

Eft's breath had given a deeply satisfying catch, his head tilting. "Really?" he asked, almost tentative. "That's really... something you'd want?"

The hunger was again flashing across his eyes, his tooth actually biting his lip, betraying a surprising glimpse of that innocence. Of how he'd never done any of this with a human, let alone with a greedy, shameless, seed-loving orc.

"Fuck, yes," Kesst whispered back, his own breath hitching. "The more of that sweet seed you can pour into me, Eft—or onto me—the fatter and happier I will be. I want those massive bollocks working for me every damned day. I want to be *reeking* of you. *Always.*"

And oh, the way the craving kept flaring in Eft's eyes, his tooth again biting his lip. "You already do," he breathed. "Smell of me, now, with the others. *Me.*"

There was unmistakable wonder in his voice, in his eyes—but curse it, that mention of others, others like *Skald*, was suddenly twisting hard and cold in Kesst's belly. Enough that he had to drop his gaze, fight to keep his smile pasted on, try not to let Eft see. Because yes, yes, gods damn it, Kesst was still a scent-stained tart, he was still tainted and weak and broken. And once again, he was completely losing his head over yet another nice cock, over a good bellyful of seed. Over an orc actually wanting his touch, wanting to taste him, and smell of him. And surely Eft was just—he was just—

"Hey," cut in Eft's voice, stronger than it had been yet, snapping up Kesst's ashamed, blinking eyes. "Perfect, Kesst. Beautiful. *Fallegur. Stórglæsilegur.* And how do I say, *I will never, ever forget this?*"

And why did Eft keep doing this, keep comforting Kesst like this, shattering him when he was supposed to be the one shattered, and Kesst swallowed hard, and attempted a smile at his face. "*Ég mun aldrei gleyma þessu,*" he whispered. "Or maybe, *ég elska þig.*"

It meant, *I adore you,* and it was once again Kesst being a greedy, needy, pathetic fool—but oh, the way Eft was smiling, like he really didn't care, he didn't. "*Ég elska þig,* Kesst," he whispered back. "I'm so glad you're here. Stay with me?"

Stay with him. For now, he surely meant, not for always, not with everything that was sure to come next—but even so, Kesst's heart was skipping, swooping, shattering again. And when Eft drew him close, right into his bloody chest, Kesst didn't even hesitate. Just curled up against him, and breathed in deep.

14

When Kesst's awareness next returned, it was to the feel of Eft's hands. Eft's strong, gentle hands, carefully shifting Kesst sideways on the floor, and then releasing him again. And then Eft's warm body was gone, and there was only the sound of his voice, speaking low and urgent. Speaking about—about *Skald*?

Kesst snapped to full wakefulness, shoving up onto his bare arse—and found himself blinking up at a bemused-looking Grimarr. Who was standing together with Eft, and now glancing back and forth between them with rapidly increasing disbelief in his eyes.

"Ach, and our brothers all *slept* through this?" he was saying to Eft, waving around at the room of unconscious orcs. "I ken this may help with their healing, but you shall *no more* do this, ach? Why else do you ken I sent them to you?"

Kesst had been intently studying Eft, the way he seemed to be easily standing, his hand absently rubbing against his now-bared chest. Which was still streaked with blood, and marred by a long, thin red line where Skald had sliced him—but even so, Kesst couldn't find a trace of pain in Eft's scent, or on his face. And instead he was looking almost sheepish, his eyes glancing briefly, helplessly, toward Kesst.

Kesst's relief—his affection, his *awe*—seemed to swarm up all at once, so strong he nearly felt dizzy with it. Eft had truly done it, he'd healed himself, he was standing here whole and well again. And not only that, but Kesst had sucked him off, they'd slept together all night, and even at this distance, Kesst could still smell his own scent on Eft, and most of all on his wry, supple mouth. On where Eft had said, *I'm so glad you're here. Ég elska þig.*

Kesst belatedly pushed up to his feet, wincing as he straightened out his stiff body, and stalked over toward Eft. Stepping close against his side, inhaling deep—gods, he smelled so, so *good* like this—and then shivering all over at the feel of Eft's arm easily, willingly, slipping around his bare waist, and drawing him closer. Wanting him here.

"Look, have you ever *met* these blockheads you sent us?" Kesst demanded flatly toward Grimarr, as he slid his own arm around Eft's back, too. "Eft had no choice but to shut them up, or else we'd both have gone mad from all their incessant griping!"

Eft's glance down at Kesst was so warm, so grateful, sending more shivers up Kesst's spine—but before them, Grimarr loudly snorted, and shook his head. "Ach, I shall grant you Silfast or Olarr, mayhap," he countered, "but Abjorn? *Drafli*? Drafli cannot even speak aloud!"

Eft was looking even more sheepish than before, rubbing at the back of his neck with his other hand, while the hand still behind Kesst fired a rueful little flare of magic into his skin. And far too late, Kesst realized that Eft had intentionally kept all these orcs asleep—clearly with a shocking amount of force, judging by their still-unconscious states—in order to keep spending time with... with him?

"You cannot *possibly* expect Eft to remember who talks, and who doesn't," Kesst belatedly pointed out, as airily as he could. "He is very busy working *miracles* down here in Ka-esh hell on our behalf, and therefore he is *fully* justified in doing whatever he damn well pleases with these infuriating imbeciles!"

Grimarr was glancing back and forth between Kesst and Eft again, now with an expression that was somewhere between aggrieved and amused. "Before this, mayhap," he said, with a sigh. "But henceforth, they stay awake. I seek to keep you both *safe*."

His gaze had dropped to the still-visible wound on Eft's chest, his eyes narrowing. And that was surely anger, studding through his scent—and perhaps even a whispering twitch of fear, too. Fear that suddenly seemed to catch and flare in Kesst's belly, in his surging circling thoughts.

Skald. Skald would remember, and return. Soon. And when he did, they would die.

"We aren't safe here," Kesst said, his voice sharp, his head shaking. "We'll never be safe here again, Grim. *Ever*."

Grimarr blinked at Kesst, his heavy brow furrowing. "Ach, not if you keep all my best fighters asleep," he said, "but Skald has spoken no more of you today, so I ken—"

"No," Kesst broke in, even sharper. "No. You don't understand, Grim. I—I sent Skald away. He doesn't—remember, yet. But he *will*."

Kesst's eyes were pleading on Grimarr's now, begging him not to make him say this aloud. Because while he'd never told Grimarr the full extent of his gift, Grimarr had surely held *some* suspicions, being the clever mistrustful arse that he was—and yes, that was comprehension, flaring in Grimarr's face. In how his eyes squeezed shut, his breath exhaling in a low, bitter growl.

"Ach, brother," he replied, quiet. "How much time, then?"

Kesst's guilt was surging, scraping, because with this, he'd surely just destroyed that grand plan of Grimarr's, whatever the hell it had been. *This healer may alter all for us...*

But this was about Eft's life. And suddenly nothing else mattered, nothing, but this. Keeping Eft safe. Returning his gift, and his promise. Repaying all the kindness Eft had so generously shown him.

"There's no time," Kesst said, his voice clipped and sure. "We need to run. Today."

15

They needed to run.

Kesst had never, ever been so certain of anything in his life, and as he stared at Grimarr's resigned eyes, he knew his best brother wouldn't argue with him on this. He'd already offered it once before, and as dangerous as it would be, running about above ground in the midst of a war, staying here would mean so much worse. It would surely mean death for him and Eft both. Likely by nightfall.

And even if there had been a chance at escaping it before—Kesst leaned a little closer into Eft, and inhaled again—now that his scent was so clearly all over Eft, and Eft's all over him, there would be no avoiding Skald's rage, or his retaliation. One single whiff of them, and Skald would know. This was the only way.

But beside Kesst, something had... changed. Something in Eft's scent, in the touch of his hand. In the strange, sudden stiffness of his warm body against him.

Kesst twitched backwards a little, looking at Eft's eyes—and found them frowning. Frowning? As if... as if he didn't...

"What do you mean, we need to *run*?" Eft said to Kesst, his voice blank. "I'm not running anywhere. Not yet."

Kesst blinked at Eft's frowning eyes, at that undeniable stubbornness swarming his scent, and he felt his own head shaking, hard. "You have to," he said. "We have to. There's no other way, Eft. If we don't, we'll *die*. Skald will murder us, just like he almost killed you yesterday. Remember?!"

And surely Eft would understand now, he would relax and nod and agree. He would say again, *I'm so glad you're here, Ég elska þig...*

But if anything, that frown on his mouth deepened, and the stubbornness in his scent swirled even harder than before. "You don't know that," he said back, his bottom lip jutting out. "I'm not running away from here like a coward, and letting that foul swine get the best of me!"

Oh. Running away, like a... a coward. And Kesst kept staring at Eft's frowning face, his body frozen in place, while something pitched and plunged in his belly. Eft was... saying no. A coward.

And perhaps Eft had followed that, his mouth grimacing, his fingers widening a little against Kesst's back. "Look, it's not that I don't appreciate your concern," he added, his voice speaking lower, faster. "Or your perspective on this. And of course you should run, if you truly want to."

Of course Kesst should. Of course he should run, like a coward. Like the coward he'd always been, perhaps. And Eft grimaced again, shaking his head, angling his frowning gaze away from Kesst, and back toward Grimarr.

"But I can't leave yet," he continued, as his frown deepened even more, and unmistakable anger seethed through his scent. "Not with this place still in such a damned mess. These orcs need help. This mountain needs help. It's a fucking *disgrace*, and whenever I think I've seen the worst of it, some new horror pops up to take its place!"

Grimarr winced, but didn't reply, and Eft stepped away

from Kesst, taking away the last of his warmth, his magic, his certainty. "This needs to be dealt with, as soon as possible," he snapped at Grimarr. "Did you not see how that scum treated Kesst? How he treated *me*?! If we treat each other like disposable *chattel*, how the hell do we treat the humans? No wonder they fear and rage against us the way they do. No wonder they want to *destroy* us!"

He'd given a furious wave down at his own scarred body as he'd spoken, and Grimarr was still looking visibly pained, his hand rubbing at his eyes. But still not speaking, not arguing this, and amidst the bitter sickness roiling in Kesst's belly, he found himself stepping forward too, his arms tightly folding over his chest, hiding his hammering heart.

"Leave him alone," he hissed at Eft, his voice brittle. "You haven't been here. You haven't seen how damned hard he's tried, how much he's done for the rest of us. It's so fucking easy to walk in from the outside and make your grand moralizing judgements, while we're the ones stuck living in it, and *dying* in it!"

Eft betrayed a palpable twitch, his mouth twisting, but he didn't stand down, didn't relent. "And you shouldn't be stuck in it," he snapped back. "It's ridiculous. You deserve a hell of a lot better than either this, or running for your life, and likely starving to death—or being *tortured* to death—in the middle of a war! And I am *not* about to let that vile scum ruin you any more than he already has!"

Ruin you. Ruin you, any more. And Kesst was again struck still, staring, while that sickness kept plunging in his belly, heaving, breaking. *Ruin. A coward.*

"We need to fix this," Eft was saying now, jabbing his claw toward Grimarr. "And we start *today*. Or else I start walking through this mountain, and ripping out fucking *arteries*!"

Oh. Wait. Wait. Because Eft could... do that. And suddenly Kesst's brain was swarming with the brutal, breath-stealing visions of it, of a raging Silfast falling onto his back, of every one of Grimarr's best fighters lying here unconscious for days on end. Eft could do that, he was quite possibly the most powerful orc ever to walk this mountain, and he'd never even said, because...

Ruin you, any more. Run, like a coward. From the smell of you, you've had half the orcs in that damned mountain fucking with your insides.

"Artery ripping," Kesst heard his voice say, from very far away. "Is that something you do often, then? A fun little side hobby?"

Eft was giving a regretful-looking grimace, but didn't reply, and Kesst again glanced around the room, at the silent sleeping orcs in their beds. "Or maybe you can just fuck with their brains," he said, his voice wavering. "Or ruin their lungs, or destroy their eyesight, or..."

And suddenly there was the horrifying vision of Kesst's own words, his own tale, the words he'd spat into Skald's blank eyes. *Boils that oozed and festered. Spasms that weakened his hands and feet. Darkness that clouded his sight...*

Cold, brittle terror was clawing up Kesst's back—had he seen that, had he *known*—and with it was more awareness, more certainty, striking him like a blow straight across the face.

This was why Grimarr had brought Eft here. *This* was the secret plan. Eft hadn't come to heal the orcs. He'd come to weaken them. To *kill* them.

I have searched, Grimarr had told Kesst, *for a human assassin to hire. This healer may alter all. It is only now that I...*

And gods, how had Kesst possibly missed it, with hints as obvious as those? How had he never put it together? Never thought to ask?

And of course he knew Grimarr was a paranoid secretive bastard, he'd accepted that fact long ago... but Eft? Eft had never said. Never hinted. Not once.

Suddenly Kesst felt dizzy and sick all over, and nearly about to vomit, right here on this dank little room's floor. Of course Eft hadn't told him such a crucial plan. Kesst was tainted, weak, compromised. *Ruined.* And Eft knew that, Eft had always known that—and yes, he might still fool around with Kesst, take his pleasure with a pretty, willing tart, like any orc would. But he was never going to actually confide in Kesst, or see him as an equal. Not after everything Kesst had done.

And far too late, Kesst realized that both Grimarr and Eft were looking at him, and that was because—he dragged his palm against his eye—because he was almost fucking weeping. He was standing here and weeping, because gods, he'd thought Eft—he'd thought—he'd—

And that was pity, oh gods, pity and regret in their eyes, all over their scents. Because they knew how pathetic Kesst was, how he'd do anything for some kind words and a nice cock, when in truth they saw him just like Skald did, just like Ofnir had. A needy, greedy, silly, foolish wench. A waste.

"Hey," Eft was saying now, his voice so thin, his mouth contorting. "Kesst. We need to talk, all right? I would still—if you still want to run, you should, and maybe we could—"

But Kesst was already shaking his head, and stumbling backwards, away, away. "No need to bother," he managed, "thinking about me, or what I might want, hmmm? Why don't you two just continue plotting, making all your secret plans, with all your secret skills. And I'll take myself well out of your way, and wait for Skald to come find me, like the ruined coward I am!"

Eft's eyes had widened, his mouth again twisting, his head shaking but Kesst knew the truth now, he did, he did. This was it. This was the fate he'd made for himself. Weak. Used. Destroyed. Drowning in his sins.

And without waiting for a reply, he whirled around and dashed away, alone, deep into the mountain's deadly darkness.

16

Kesst ended up in yet another tiny room, in another dank corner of Ka-esh hell.

It was a room that was far too familiar, a room that had consumed far too many of his formative years. A room that had long ago been set up like a human's, with a dusty human bed, a faded human tapestry, and even a small, rocking human cradle.

Kesst had never known how his mother had found this room, or how she'd become so attached to it—but it had somehow become her refuge, her escape. A place well out of the way, a place where Ash-Kai like his father—and like Kaugir—wouldn't often come. The air too thick, the scents too turgid, for the Ash-Kai who were accustomed to living and ruling at the very top of the mountain.

But being human, Kesst's mother had never noticed the scents, or the thickness of the air. So Kesst had borne it, choked on it, so he could stay here with her, and tell her the tales she'd loved. Tales of lords and princesses, of love known and won, of happy endings, of peace.

And if she'd wept while Kesst had told her his tales, he'd

learned to never falter, to never show pity or grief. To keep the smile pasted to his face, to keep his voice easy and light. To be the escape she'd wanted, the relief she'd so desperately craved.

But in this moment, this dark suffocating emptiness, there was no way to cover the grief, or the shame. No way to stop the sobs from escaping, and tearing out of his clogged, miserable throat, as he buried his face in the musty old bed.

Gods, how had he done this, again? How had he thrown all his hope, all his desperate loneliness, onto one stubborn impossible orc? Why had he ever thought he'd deserved even a glimmer of peace or happiness, after all he'd done?

And he'd done so damned much. Not only with Eft—not only throwing that target upon him when he hadn't deserved it—but with all these years of placating, of ingratiating, of lying. Of craving the safety, and yes, maybe even the power and status, too. Wanting to be desired, and valued, and protected. Cared for.

But in that, what had he become? What had it made him, when he'd again and again made that choice to smile, to beg, to step closer? To freely flaunt his body and his hunger? To make himself into the needy, greedy minion his oppressors had wanted? To become yet another means of displaying their strength, their superiority, their cruelty?

He was a coward. He was. And of course Eft had seen it, and known it, and called it exactly what it was. And of course a brilliant, upstanding orc like Eft didn't want any part of that. He'd seen Kesst's sins. He'd known.

But gods, it had been good. So good. Better than Grimarr, better than any of the dozens—or likely hundreds—of orcs Kesst had taken his pleasures with. And it was still so damned strong, that scent still here on his cock and his mouth, still swarming his breath. Almost as if—as if—

"Hey," said a voice, a too-familiar, too-painful voice—and

when Kesst flailed around on the bed to look, his heart thundering in his chest, it was—

Eft. Eft, here, in this room, reaching out his hand, and then pulling it back again. Like he was... reluctant. Regretful.

And it was too much, too much, and Kesst frantically flopped back onto the bed, burying his face back into his arm. "You don't need to bother," he gulped. "You can just go back to your grand plans, and your artery-ripping, and whatever the hell else you haven't told me. And"—he dragged in another breath—"don't worry, I'll still get myself out of your way, once I've got my cowardly rubbish dealt with. And you won't need to—you don't need to—"

Think of me again, he was supposed to say, but instead the words choked into something thick and shameful, something too much like a sob. And gods, he was lying here like the weak waste he was, weeping into a bed that still scented of his mother, when she'd been dead for half his damned life.

"Look, Kesst, I—I'm sorry," came Eft's voice, thin and low. "I shouldn't have implied that running makes you a coward. It doesn't. It *wouldn't*."

Kesst shook his head into his arm, because he was a coward, he *was*—and Eft made a sound like a growl, a groan. "You are not," his hard voice continued. "You aren't, Kesst. You're one of the bravest people I've ever met. The way you've dealt with Skald, it's fearless. And it's damn well terrifying, all right? I've never been so afraid of anything in all my life, I can't even tell you, Kesst, I *can't*."

His voice sounded surprisingly earnest, maybe even bleak, and Kesst could feel his hand, his magic, hovering over his back, and snatching away again. "And I'm sorry I didn't tell you," he said, his voice lower, "about the... other side of my magic. You're so clever, I thought maybe you would... you might..."

Kesst barked a brittle laugh into his arm, shaking his head, because he was not clever, clearly he wasn't, he'd never imagined Eft as a killer, not once—and he could feel Eft's sigh, thick and heavy on his bare back. "And that's me putting it on you, again," he said. "Because I also—I just—didn't want you to see me like that. Didn't want you to be—afraid of me. You've already seen so much, and faced so much, and I just—"

He broke off there, and that was another sigh, prickling against Kesst's back. "I should have told you," he continued, quieter. "I can heal people, and I can... not heal them. I know dozens of ways to bring death, or pain, or madness. I killed my first human when I was nine years old, and since then I have killed—"

He again stopped, his breath heaving out hard, and without at all meaning to, Kesst pushed up, and looked. Finding Eft sitting on the edge of the bed, his hands folded in his lap, his head bowed. His mouth tight, his scent tasting of grief, and of... guilt.

"Too many," Eft continued, so soft, toward his hands. "So many. I went through a time when I was so angry, I killed any human who raised a hand against me. Men and women both. Old and young. I was the monster they wanted me to be, and I *revelled* in it."

Kesst felt his throat swallow, but he couldn't seem to find his voice, his words—and before him, Eft barked a hoarse little laugh, his clawed fingers folding tightly together. "You haven't killed anyone," he said, even quieter. "Have you? I know the scent so well, you see, I can smell it on most of the orcs in this mountain. But you..."

He gave Kesst a brief, miserable smile, before dropping his gaze back to his hands. And Kesst couldn't seem to face it, to follow it, and he rubbed his own hands at his wet eyes, stared past Eft at the darkness beyond.

"No," he whispered, finally. "I haven't killed anyone. But I stood there and let it happen. And then"—he drew his knees to his chest, wrapped his arms tightly around them—"I found *pleasure* in what they gave me. I begged them for it, like the needy, greedy, *ruined* coward I am."

Eft's mouth twisted into another sad smile, his eyes again angling toward Kesst's. "Not a coward," he said, while a twitch of that stubbornness unfurled through the air. "And not ruined, either. I never should have said that, all right? I only meant how they've treated you, how they've hurt you, and the way it's just so—so *normal* to you. The way it's affected how you think about yourself, and talk about yourself. It's not right, Kesst, and it's not true. It *isn't.*"

Something was tilting in Kesst's chest, in his throat, but Eft was still speaking, shaking his head. "You keep talking as though you're somehow guilty," he continued, "when *they're* the ones who reek of death. *They're* the ones who trapped you here in this mess, and stole away all your other options. And so what if you found some pleasure with them? Our bodies are *made* to find pleasure, Kesst. It doesn't mean anything is wrong with you. Nothing is wrong with you. *Nothing.*"

There was truly no way to answer this, Kesst's body frozen and desperately listening on the bed, and Eft gave a heavy sigh, another regretful glance at Kesst's eyes. "And if you really want to talk about guilt," he added, his voice lowering, "I've committed a hell of a lot more sins than you have, Kesst. Dozens of times over. *You're* the innocent one in this room, all right? You're probably the most innocent orc in this entire gods-forsaken mountain. *You.*"

You. Kesst still couldn't stop staring at Eft's blank face, feeling all these impossible words jumbling through his thoughts, clanging against his ribs. *You. Made to find pleasure. The most innocent orc...*

But no. No. This cursed healer was doing it again, distracting Kesst again, breaking down all his defenses. And

Kesst had to focus, had to *think*, damn it, and he somehow managed to scoff a brittle laugh, and shake his head.

"Look, you don't need to keep playing at all this anymore, *Efterar*," he said, his voice wavering. "Even if you really *didn't* mean to call me a ruined coward, the truth of it is, you still lied to me. You didn't think I deserved to know the truth about your magic, even after I told you about mine. Even after I told Skald that... *tale*."

The chills were streaking up his spine again, his shoulders hunching, his eyes dropping. "And you damn well did not tell me," he continued, "why you actually came here. Why you'd even bother coming here, when you already had your own life elsewhere, with no connection whatsoever to this hellhole. Let me guess"—his voice hardened—"Grim probably brought you here on a term, right? Offered you plenty of gold? Maybe a pretty, willing wench or two? In exchange for what, Skald's death? Or Kaugir's, too?"

There was utter, empty silence from Eft, ringing with over-powering weight between them, and when Kesst finally glanced up, Eft's face looked markedly pale, his throat visibly bobbing. "Not Kaugir's," he whispered. "Just Skald's."

Gods damn it. Damn Grimarr and Eft both, because even if Kesst had already known it, the bare spoken truth of it still seemed to strike him to horrible, miserable stillness. Eft had been Grimarr's assassin. And neither one of them had said. Neither one of them had trusted Kesst to know.

"But look, I've fucked it up, all right?" Eft continued, his voice rising. "Skald almost immediately mistrusted me, and I keep losing my temper with the foul swine, and haven't once been able to get close enough to touch him without raising suspicion. And now there's *you*, and now I have a very clear motive for doing it, and that puts us all at risk. And I'm not even sure how I can possibly do it anymore, and now we only have this one day left, and—"

He'd been speaking very quickly, his eyes darting briefly toward Kesst, and away again. While Kesst still felt only cold, desolate stillness, his gaze frozen on Eft's pale profile. Because not only had Eft never trusted him... but now it was *his* fault that Eft had failed? *His* fault that Skald was still alive? His fault that Skald had immediately mistrusted Eft...

Gods, what had Kesst done. How had he managed to ruin so much. And how the hell could he possibly fix this, how could he ever face himself again, what did he possibly have left...

This. Just this.

His trembling hand had somehow found Eft's shoulder, his fingers spreading wide—and Eft's glance at him was startled, surprised. But he wasn't moving away, his throat again convulsing, and Kesst shifted closer, let his hand slide down Eft's broad bare back.

"You'll find a way," he murmured, as smoothly as he could. "You're completely brilliant, love, and the most stubborn orc I've ever met. And you're right, I should have guessed all this, but now it all makes perfect sense, of course. And of course running away doesn't make sense either, if dealing with Skald directly has been your plan all along, hmmm?"

Something shifted in Eft's eyes, something Kesst couldn't quite read, but he kept stroking, moving slightly behind Eft's big body, now rubbing both hands at his stiff shoulders. "And I guarantee you," he continued, keeping the smile on his face so Eft could still hear it, "Ol' Grim is probably over there frantically whipping up plots as we speak, and he'll likely show up back here with some fully formed master plan at any moment. And gods only know if you got a wink of sleep last night, what with you almost *dying* on me. So you should relax for a little while, love, and lie back, and let me take care of you."

And yes, yes, it was working, Kesst could just see Eft's eyes fluttering closed, his tooth biting his lip. And when

Kesst gently pulled at his shoulders, guiding him down toward the bed, Eft willingly went, and heavily sagged onto his back. Indeed looking truly exhausted, suddenly, what with the dark circles beneath his bleary eyes, the faint new lines around his mouth. But Kesst kept that smile on his face, kept his gaze warm and light on Eft's, kept his scent as steady as he could.

"Good," he murmured. "Just like that, love. Now tell me, what would you like most? Maybe you'll let me ride that gorgeous prick of yours? Let me feel it rearrange my insides?"

Eft's tired eyes fluttered again, a low, betraying growl hissing from his throat—and Kesst's brief glance downwards indeed confirmed it, that still-shocking length prominently straining beneath his trousers. And when Kesst's hand flitted down against it, it pressed powerfully up in return. Still wanting him, still wanting this from him, if nothing else.

"Good," Kesst purred again, flashing Eft his best, hungriest smile, as he brought his other hand to his own rapidly swelling cock, still blatantly bared at his groin. "You know I've been dreaming about this, love. Wanting to feel you inside me. Wanting you to flood me so full of your seed, I never, *ever* stop smelling of you."

Eft's answering moan sounded helpless this time, strangled, his head slightly shaking. "You don't," he croaked, "still *want* that."

But Kesst was still smiling, holding it all steady, holding it all in. "Of course I do," he whispered, as he wrapped his hand tighter around his own shaft, and stroked up its full hardened length. "I want anything you'll give me, love. I'll do *anything*."

But wait. No. That was the wrong thing, the wrong words— because Eft's body beneath Kesst had suddenly twitched to rigid, unnatural stillness. His eyes rapidly narrowing, his jaw clenching—and without warning he'd sat back up again, his face thrusting into Kesst's neck, his breath purposefully inhaling, while his hand spread wide against Kesst's bare chest. His magic unfurling deep within, seeking, searching, knowing...

And finding. Finding the rapid pace of Kesst's heart. The tension in his lungs, the effort it was taking to breathe. The seething sickness in his stomach. All the misery still there in his body, even if he'd somehow managed to hide it on his face, on his scent.

And suddenly Eft was reeling away, lurching up, his magic wrenching out behind him. Leaving Kesst sitting there bared and shamefully aroused on the bed, and staring blankly after him.

"Gods damn it, Kesst," Eft hissed, without turning around, his shoulders rising and falling in an unsteady rhythm. "What the hell. You think I want that rubbish? Want you wheedling and simpering and playing up to me, like I'm *him*? The *fuck*!"

The anger was wheeling through Eft's scent now, whirling out behind him like yet another strike, and Kesst felt his face whipping sideways, away, the misery swarming up in a blaring, overpowering flood. And there were so many words, *I'm sorry, I need to try, I need to make it up to you, I need to do something, to be something, to try to salvage this, to feel this before we die today...*

But none of it would seem to come out, and Eft still wasn't looking at him, churning up the despair even darker, colder. "You do want it," Kesst's hollow voice finally said. "Because if you really wanted me, why wouldn't you trust me? You know I'd have kept it secret, I'm good at secrets even under duress, I'd never have told."

Eft didn't reply, didn't look, so Kesst kept saying it, his voice faded and bleak. "I could have helped you," he whispered. "Instead of fucking it up at every possible turn. But this"—he gave a shaky wave at his bared body that Eft couldn't see—"*this* is the help you wanted, the help you need, from the pretty wench Grim promised you. So of course I want to give it to you, want to give you *anything*."

His voice wavered into the silence, into the wall of Eft's stiff back, and those shoulders rose and fell again, heavier this time. "Grimarr did not," Eft finally said, his voice very tight, "promise me *you*."

But Kesst's laugh escaped on its own, his head shaking. "And it *never* crossed either of your devious minds," his thin voice said, "that with Skald out of the way, I'd be looking for a big, powerful, well-hung new orc to simper and wheedle and play up to? *Really*, Eft, you obviously know me *that* well, at least, don't you?"

Eft's groan was thick and hoarse, his hands dragging against his hair—and he abruptly whirled around again, and came a swift step toward Kesst. "Stop that," he said, his voice cracking. "I can't bear you talking about yourself that way. You're brave and clever and beautiful and impossibly gifted, all right? And I didn't tell you the truth because *I* was the coward, Kesst. *I* was. I was terrified of this. Of *this*."

He'd flapped his hand between them, his mouth twisting, the bitterness curdling through his scent. "I never wanted you to think this was all some kind of ploy, or that I was using you to get to *him*," he said. "I never wanted you to think I had some ulterior motive for healing you, or touching you, or spending time with you. And I also didn't want to give you any false hope, or make you feel like you needed to do anything, or owe me anything. In truth, I should have kept my distance from you altogether, kept you entirely out of it, but—"

The bitterness in his scent had condensed, sharpened, his eyes shifting and shining on Kesst's. "But," he said, with a sigh, as he came another step closer. "Ever since that first day we met, I've never wanted anyone else, never wanted anything so much. I couldn't believe my eyes when I saw you, all right? Couldn't believe how good you smelled, couldn't stop wondering how you'd taste. You're so damned stunning, Kesst, *fallegur*, *stórglæsilegur*, blameless, pure, perfect. Whatever the hell you need me to say, I'll say it. I'm so sorry, Kesst, and *ég elska þig. Ég elska þig.*"

A furious shudder chased up Kesst's back, and he blinked hard, heard himself bark a distant, brittle laugh. "You don't even know," he croaked, "what that means."

But Eft's eyes didn't even flicker, and he closed the last distance between them, his hand slowly rising, very carefully stroking along Kesst's cheek. "I love you," he whispered back. "That has to be what it means. Right?"

Kesst's laugh sounded more like a sob this time, his head shaking. "You barely even know me," he choked. "It's been how long, a—"

But his voice broke there, his fear suddenly soaring, obliterating all else. Because once again, a familiar, horrible scent was charging down from the direction of the Ash-Kai rooms, coming closer and closer...

Skald, damn it, *Skald*. And with him, a good half-dozen other Ash-Kai and Skai, too. Coming for them. *Fuck.*

Kesst's terror surged up higher, his head wildly shaking, his eyes angling toward the door. Because no matter what Skald remembered, no matter where things stood, this still meant their certain doom. Because the instant Skald smelled what they'd done, it was over, over, forever—

"We have to run," Kesst gulped at Eft, suddenly clinging to his arm, pleading at his eyes. "We have to. It's the only way. Please."

But curse the stubborn bastard, Eft wasn't moving, he was just standing there, his jaw set, his gaze glittering on Kesst's face. "I can't," he breathed. "As long as that swine lives, and has you in his scents, you're in danger. I need to do this, Kesst, need to keep you safe. I need to try."

Kesst kept frantically shaking his head, flailing his hands, hot terror prickling at his eyes, screeching up his back. "And I need you to *not die!*" he shot back. "You gods-damned menace, you can't keep doing this to me, I can't watch him hurt you again, I'm—"

Eft's skittering hands were both on Kesst's face now, his thumbs firmly wiping away the wetness pooling beneath his eyes. "You're one of the bravest people I've ever met," he whispered. "And now that you know everything"—he drew away a little, his throat audibly swallowing—"will you help me? Please?"

Would Kesst... help. And blinking at the fervent urgency in Eft's eyes, Kesst realized that this was Eft... trying to fix this. Trying to be honest. Trying to show Kesst what he truly did want from him. *Will you help me.*

And surely it was their death, it was their devastation, their certain and unrelenting doom—but Kesst somehow, somehow nodded.

"Yes," he whispered. "Yes, Eft. Anything."

17

E ft's answering nod was firm and forceful, his relief swarming through his scent. And without another word, he abruptly clasped Kesst's hand, and pulled him toward the door.

"What are you doing," Kesst hissed, as Eft drew him out and down the cramped corridor, straight toward the rising, rapidly approaching scents and sounds of Skald and his band of minions. "Why are you—"

But within a breath, Eft had swung Kesst back against the corridor's cool stone wall, leaned in close, and... kissed him. His mouth heated and hungry on Kesst's, his big body boxing him in, his groin grinding hard against Kesst's still-bare hips.

"Need him to touch me," Eft whispered, as he briefly pulled away, his tongue brushing his parted lips. "More likely to happen in a small space. And if this is it for me, well—"

He shrugged, and then pressed his mouth back against Kesst's, shoving him even tighter to the wall. And even as Kesst eagerly arched into his kiss, groaning into Eft's mouth, he somehow felt himself twitching back again, long enough to drag in a shaky lungful of air.

"And when you touch him, you'll do what," he breathed, holding Eft's flaring eyes. "Tear his arteries?"

Kesst couldn't have said why he wanted to know, why it mattered so much—but he suddenly, desperately needed to hear Eft say it. Needed Eft to keep telling him the truth, making him part of this, even as Skald's scent marched closer, closer...

"Whatever I can," Eft whispered back, speaking very quickly and quietly now, his gaze angling uneasily down the corridor. "Heart's easiest to hide, but takes longer. If not that, then probably this."

He'd brushed his thumb against the pulse in Kesst's neck, meeting his eyes with a grimace. Almost as if he expected Kesst to cower, or shy away—but instead, Kesst found himself fervently, gratefully nodding, and dragging Eft close again. Crushing their mouths back together with reckless purpose, and moaning into the sweet, answering eagerness of Eft's lips and tongue and teeth. Into how the brash sloppiness of the kiss was already changing, shifting into something more certain, Eft reading Kesst's body as easily as if it had been his own.

Gods, it was good, and even better when Eft's strong hands swiftly dropped, grasping Kesst's bare arse, and hitching it up. So Kesst could wrap his long legs around Eft's waist, his arms tightening around his neck, his fingers sinking into his hair. While their mouths kept tasting, biting, drinking as though they were drowning. And almost forgetting, almost, if only for a moment...

"Ach, there he is," growled a booming, horrible voice, scraping like claws down Kesst's spine. "And what is *this*?!"

This, surely, was them, the way Eft was blatantly grinding Kesst into the wall, the way they both reeked of seed and desire, the way Kesst was still entirely unclothed, with his own swollen prick brazenly bared between them. And the way— gods help him—Kesst had reluctantly drawn away from Eft's kiss, his heart hammering, his eyes blinking with genuine haziness toward Skald's furious, rapidly approaching face.

This was it. He wasn't hiding this time. Wasn't cowering. He wasn't.

"Oh, hello, Skald," he made his voice say, as he flagrantly rocked his hips, grinding himself against the length of Eft's magnificent prick. "Can we catch up later? Just a *bit* busy at the moment."

There were a few shocked gasps from Skald's entourage, and even Skald himself had reeled back a little, his mouth dropping open, his eyes flaring with rage. His hand already clutching the hilt of the scimitar at his side, oh *hell*—but wait, here were more orcs' scents, charging up the corridor. Grimarr, and Abjorn, and Silfast and Olarr, and Drafli, and Grimarr's other shadow Baldr, too. Witnesses from each clan, Kesst's distant brain couldn't help noting, as he gave another slow, succulent roll of his hips against Eft's, pressing their cocks together, and driving a satisfyingly genuine growl from Eft's mouth.

"You fickle little wench," Skald barked, yanking out his scimitar in a flash of steel, and striding closer with deadly, purposeful steps. "How dare you scorn me thus! After all you have already done?!"

Kesst attempted his best wide-eyed look, even as Eft—the menace—bent his head into Kesst's neck, and *nipped* him. Not hard, but just *perfect*, with one of those glorious little splashes of magic from his tongue, and Kesst's answering moan wasn't even slightly feigned, his body arching closer against Eft's, his head tipping back against the wall, willing Eft to do that again. And devious bastard that he was, Eft did, as Kesst wrenched and writhed against him.

"Not *scorning*," Kesst replied, between heavy breaths. "Just—having a bit of fun, like you always do. Never thought we were ever—*exclusive*, were we?"

He was studying Skald's furious face from beneath his fluttering lashes, and realizing, with a twitch of surprise, that Skald
was surely still under the spell of his tale. That yes, yes, he had
to be, the way he was slightly hesitating, his eyes darting
toward Eft. But his scimitar hadn't lifted, not yet, and Eft had to
touch, he'd said, and Kesst had to help. *Anything...*

"But I will admit," Kesst blithely continued, tossing his hair
over his shoulder, "that you were right after all, Skald dearest,
and this stuffy grump healer has actually proven *far* more
tempting than I originally anticipated. Saved my life, you know,
when you were too busy to bother. And have you *seen* his
prick?"

And was he really doing this, he was dropping a hand down
between them, and stroking up that hard, beautiful length in
Eft's trousers. All while keeping his cool eyes on Skald's rapidly
reddening face, and what else would set him raging, what else
might push him over the edge...

"And you know, Skald dearest, I wouldn't even mind
swearing vows to this one," he said, ignoring the odd twitch
from Eft against him. "Making myself his for *life*, because with
a prick and skills like this, who needs anything else? And
surely you'd give me your blessing, Skald, wouldn't you? I know
you have plenty of other adoring orcs to—"

But it was that, finally, that sent Skald charging forward,
and crashing into them. Knocking Eft out of the way with his
shoulder, sending him staggering backwards, away—and now
it was only Skald here, Skald pinning Kesst to the wall, his
body huge and horrifying, his sweet breath hot and sickening
in Kesst's face.

"I tire of your games, you babbling little wench," he hissed,
as his powerful hand came up, and curled around Kesst's neck.
"Now beg me for my mercy, and my strong ploughing!"

His minions had crowded in behind him, several of them
roughly yanking Eft further away, no, no, no—because Skald

was still standing here, still perfectly healthy and whole, still ready to squeeze the life out of Kesst at any moment. And Kesst couldn't dare attempt a tale now, the world was already going hazy before his eyes...

No. They'd failed. They'd taken such a stupid, reckless risk and they'd failed...

And Kesst couldn't even seem to find any words, suddenly, between the tightness on his throat, the clamping deep inside it. He'd tried so hard, and he'd failed, he should have known it would never have worked, he would never be able to actually help, he was...

"Now!" Skald roared into Kesst's face, as something slightly shifted, shuddered, in his eyes. "*Now*, you lying little cheat, before I—"

His eyes had shifted again, changing in a way that Kesst knew so, so well, and the panic had truly started screaming now, tearing against his thoughts. Skald's awareness was coming back, he was about to remember everything, he would make this slow and agonizing and then he would do it to Eft and—

And Eft. Eft, still struggling against the orcs holding him, his eyes blazing on Kesst's. With fear, and with urgency, and with... purpose. With vivid, desperate purpose, as his hand lurched up to his own neck, and... squeezed. Hard, purposeful, there. Just against his pulse, just where he'd touched Kesst only moments before...

Kesst's vision was wildly spinning now, his thoughts faltering, but he dragged in one last, frantic breath, and somehow, somehow nodded. Nodded, and found his tingling hands, and even attempted a wavering smile toward Skald's reeking, enraged face.

"Very well," he croaked, against Skald's ever-tightening grip on his throat, as he settled his numb-feeling hands on Skald's face. A gesture of intimacy, of ingratiation, of a wheedling and simpering orc who knew very well when he was defeated...

And with all the strength left in his fingers, he pressed. Pressed just where Eft had shown him, just against Skald's powerfully thudding pulse, and then held it, and smiled. And shivered, and kept smiling, and somehow even found his breath again, because had Skald's grip on his neck loosened, just a little?

"Very well," Kesst said again, still smiling. "I must beg your forgiveness, Skald dearest. Of course I hadn't the slightest intention of disrespecting you, or the foggiest expectation that you should even take time out of your *very* busy schedule to show up back here in Ka-esh hell anyway. And if you truly feel that strongly about me, I—*ack!*"

Because at that moment, Skald's hand had fully slipped from Kesst's neck, his eyes rolling back, his head slightly tilting—

And then he sagged downwards, and sprawled to the floor at Kesst's feet.

18

For a hushed, hanging instant, no one moved. No one but Skald, his huge body twitching on the floor, his eyes still rolled back, his claws scraping at the stone...

And then... silence. And the distinct scent of urine, growing ever stronger in the air. As Kesst's shaking hands finally flitted up to cover his mouth, his eyes frozen on the sight at his feet.

"What—what happened?" he said blankly, with genuine-sounding shock in his voice. "Was he—was he shot?"

He glanced frantically around the crowded corridor, as if searching for an errant lurking human with a crossbow, and thankfully many of the surrounding orcs began to do the same. Not only Skald's orcs, but Grimarr's, too—though when Kesst's eyes caught on Grimarr himself, Grimarr was looking straight back toward him. And in those familiar eyes, that was surely a flash of pure, gleeful, unfettered triumph.

We did it, they said. *You did it, brother.*

But then it was gone again, as Grimarr rushed down to kneel at Skald's side, putting a hand to his throat. "His heart has stopped," he said, curt and authoritative. "Efterar! Come here, at once!"

Eft swiftly obliged, and in the lurching, jumbled moments that followed, he and Grimarr delivered a highly impressive performance, displaying only the utmost urgency and concern for Skald's welfare. Attempting and failing to re-start his heart, searching in vain for other possible solutions, and then calling for Kaugir. And luckily—or rather, conspicuously—Kaugir had still been up in the Ash-Kai rooms, enjoying an elaborate meal with the rest of his minions, and by the time his huge bulk stalked into the crowded corridor, the tale was already spun and set among all the surrounding witnesses.

Our Left Hand's heart stopped. Worked himself too hard in the arena today, mayhap. Gaining more years than we knew. Even the new bewitcher could not help him. A grave mishap.

And also, much, much quieter, *Shocked to see his silly wench take up with another orc. Ought to have known. Might have been kinder.*

But it was Grimarr who again told the full tale to his father, his voice and eyes dark and solemn. Focusing most of all on Skald's bout of unexpected rage, but also on Kesst's eagerness to oblige him, and all the various valiant efforts they'd made at reviving their fallen Left Hand. A sad account that was willingly defended by all the witnesses present, even Skald's own orcs.

It was a truly masterful display, but Kesst's own heart had kept skipping as Grimarr had spoken, his eyes firmly fixed to Kaugir's heavy, unreadable face. What would he do. What would he say. Was this the end...

But then Kaugir finally shrugged, and spun and lumbered away, with his hangers-on scurrying close at his heels. And watching them go, Kesst very nearly lost his footing entirely, sagging back against the wall behind him, his eyes again frozen on Skald's limp body at his feet. The body he'd known so well, the body he'd killed.

Skald was gone. Gone forever. Because of... him. Because of

Eft. *Help me*, Eft had said, and Kesst had done it. Gods above, he'd done it.

"Hey," murmured a familiar voice, and with it, a familiar brush of magic into his bare back. "Kesst. Come with me?"

Kesst silently nodded, suddenly not quite able to meet Eft's eyes, but he willingly clasped his hand, and followed. Followed him back down the corridor again, back into his mother's old, abandoned room. And when Eft nudged him down onto his back on the bed, Kesst willingly did that too, blinking hazily up at how Eft had settled on top of him, his upper body propped on his elbows, his eyes alarmingly bright on Kesst's face.

"You brilliant, beautiful wonder," Eft breathed, his chest heaving warm and shaky against Kesst's. "You miracle. You *marvel*. You *saved* us."

Kesst's numb-feeling body had somehow begun shivering, his head twitching back and forth. "That was you," he whispered back. "You, Eft. I was sure you couldn't pull it off, he scarcely even touched you, he—"

He couldn't finish, the bare blaring fear of that moment churning through his belly, but already Eft's magic was there, soothing it again. "I almost didn't," he said. "At least, not fast enough to keep him from killing us—but when you compressed that artery for me, you fixed it. *Finished* it."

Kesst was still shivering, the shock and the chaos still sweeping up and down the full length of his body, but Eft's magic kept following it, settling it again. "And you played it so beautifully, Kesst, you fearless terrifying *hellion*. I swear"—his voice cracked, his forehead lowering to gently bump against Kesst's—"you nearly stopped my own heart a dozen times over. I am *never* going to recover from that."

Kesst felt himself gulp a laugh, his head shaking against Eft's. "Me neither," he managed. "I—I *k-killed* him, Eft."

Eft's exhale was harsh but warm against Kesst's face, his eyes briefly closing. "I'm so sorry it ended up being you, instead of me," he whispered back. "I'm sorry I took that from you. But"—he drew away a little again, his gaze flashing on Kesst's—"he deserved it. And if we'd had more time, I would have damn well made every word of your tale come true. I would have made that swine suffer, and I'd have *laughed* to watch him weep and plead for his death. He was never, *ever* touching you like that again. *Never*, Kesst."

The pure, vicious vehemence in his voice sent another hard shudder up Kesst's spine, enough that Eft grimaced, clearly regretting betraying all that—but in Kesst's stilted, stuttering thoughts, there was the vague realization that he didn't actually care. He didn't care how brutal Eft was to anyone else, as long as he was kind to him. Honest with him. And maybe even treated him as a partner, after all.

"You don't *always* run around killing people, though, do you?" Kesst heard his voice ask, as his trembling arms belatedly slid up around Eft's broad back, clinging tight to its strength. "The healing really is still your calling, right? Your gift?"

He was thinking back to what Eft had told him that day he'd carried him home, what felt like many moons before—and Eft was already nodding, fervent and quick. "I hadn't for years," he whispered. "I refused Grimarr on this job multiple times. But then he started telling me tales, tales about orcs like *you*, and I—"

He winced and shook his head, and Kesst stroked his hands up and down his back, clutching him even tighter. "It was so good of you to come help us," he murmured. "Do you—do you think you might still—go away again, though? Now that this is—"

He couldn't finish, the thought of Eft leaving—*leaving*—sending more horrible convulsions to his stomach. But bless Eft, the magic was already there again, knowing him too well, seeing him, saving him.

"Was thinking I'd rather stay," Eft whispered now, so soft,

his eyes shifting on Kesst's. "You see, there's this stunning, *stór-glæsilegur* orc here. And he's so quick and clever, he makes me laugh, he makes everything feel lighter and easier. And he's so generous and open-hearted, he's never held my fool mouth against me, even when I damn well deserve it. And he's a brilliant cook and an even better lover, and he keeps saying all these unthinkable things he wants to do to me, and I"—he hesitated, drew in an unsteady breath—"I can't leave you, Kesst. You've been a marvel, and such a gift, and I'm so, so sorry I hurt you with all this. I love you. *Ég elska þig.*"

Kesst's smile was trembling on his lips, his hands trembling on Eft's back, his hair. "You don't know that," he breathed. "You can't, Eft. It's only been—"

"Long enough," Eft cut in, quiet but firm, while that familiar stubbornness studded into his scent, his eyes, his mouth. "I've made up my mind, all right? And that's not changing. Not unless you say no."

Oh. And despite everything, despite all the possible questions and protests Kesst could have attempted, he found himself swallowing, holding Eft's stubborn gaze. Letting himself sink into the impossible possibility of it, even just for a moment.

"You know I'd never say no," Kesst finally whispered, as his quivering hands kept distantly caressing, wandering as they willed. "You know I've been hopelessly attached to you ever since you carried me home. Told me you wouldn't toss me in the thicket. And that you didn't want any sons."

Eft huffed a choked-sounding laugh, shaking his head against Kesst's hands. "The sons, huh?" he said, so soft. "Didn't realize that was a factor in the slightest."

Kesst's hands were stroking against Eft's scarred cheeks, up to the tips of his ears, deep into his hair against his scalp. Still in its braid, always in its braid, and Kesst's fingers were pulling it out, because maybe he could, he could. "Of course it was," he said thickly. "I mean, it's not that I don't *like* orclings, I'd happily be an uncle or something—but I don't want to *have* one. Don't want to share you with one. I want you to just want... *me.*"

It sounded appallingly selfish, and surely now Eft would pull away, he'd realize his ghastly mistake. And it would feel even worse now, because Kesst had finished pulling out Eft's braid, and his waves of silken black hair had fallen around his face, flooding Kesst with more of his succulent scent, more of his dark beautiful safety. Gods, he was the most gorgeous orc Kesst had ever seen in his life, and he was nearly whimpering at the sight of it, here, nearly within his grasp...

"Just you," came Eft's voice, sending a deep, thundering thrill up the full length of Kesst's body. A thrill that was instantly chased by a stunning sweep of Eft's magic, following it, resonating out against it in strange, shimmering harmony. *Just you.*

And it almost felt like it was... changing Kesst. Remaking him. Transforming him into something he couldn't ever remember being before, something bright and bare and true. Something wanted, trusted, honoured. Something... safe.

And it was filling Kesst, it was flooding him to his bones, to his heart. And there was only one part missing, one last crucial bit left, and Kesst abruptly gripped Eft with his arms and legs, and rolled him over onto his back. Sprawling him wide on the bed, his hair a black halo around his head, his tooth already biting at his lip. Wanting this, Eft wanted him, and Kesst sat up over him with smooth, easy gracefulness, and felt his mouth curve into a slow, genuine smile.

"Then show me, love," he murmured. "And fill me with you, until I damn well *burst.*"

19

E ft's shudder was hard, wrenching, and thoroughly gratifying, rippling all the way through his sprawled body. His muscles taut and hungry, his glorious prick already straining against his trousers, pulsing up between Kesst's bared, spread legs. And his scent was pure barrelling hunger, ready to drive deep into Kesst, to make him his, once and for all.

But Eft's shaky hand had come to Kesst's knee, squeezing with both a flare of magic, and a gentle bite of claws. Dragging Kesst to sudden, breathless stillness upon him, a hint of the old uncertainty rising, returning...

"You're—sure," Eft's voice croaked, his breaths panting. "*Sure* you want it. No pretending. No exaggerating. No doing something because you think it's what *I* want."

Kesst felt himself grimace, because yes, he'd probably deserved that—but he held Eft's eyes as he slowly, purposefully dropped his hand to his own groin, stroking up the full length of his rock-hard, already-dripping prick. "I want it," he whispered back, as he squeezed out a thick bead of seed, and then another. Felt it drop and dangle, longer and longer, until it caught on the skin of Eft's bare torso. Connecting them, binding them, in a sweet-scented string of white.

"I want it," Kesst said again, stronger this time, as he stroked up harder, thickened that liquid touch. "I always have, you know. Because I'm a—"

Eft's eyes—which had been very intent on what Kesst was doing—had flashed upwards to his face, matched by another meaningful flare of magic into his knee. And Kesst felt his throat swallow, his mouth giving a rueful, affectionate little smile.

"Because I'm yours," he said softly, and that still felt true, it was. "Need to make it real. Need to feel you inside me."

Eft audibly gulped, his eyes fluttering hard, and Kesst's smile felt even warmer, brighter, as he dropped his other hand to Eft's trousers, yanking them downwards. Releasing that long, hungry, stunning cock, with Kesst's scent still so fresh and powerful upon it.

Gods, it was gorgeous, it was perfection, *he* was perfection. And Kesst should take his good time with this, he should take Eft apart piece by piece under his touch... but his mouth was dry, his head was spinning, the craving slamming so hard he felt faint. He needed this. Needed this so damned much. Now.

"Need you inside me," he gulped at Eft, or perhaps pleaded. "More than anything, Eft. Need you to impale me on you, and flood me so full of your seed, it's coming up out my *throat.*"

Eft's guttural moan sounded just as frantic as Kesst felt, that hard length already bobbing upwards, brushing Kesst's hanging bollocks. And suddenly they were both scrabbling, Kesst shifting up and forward, Eft taking his prick in hand, and guiding it up. His other hand catching on Kesst's hip, Kesst's hands gripping back against Eft's thighs as he arched and opened himself, relaxed himself, lowered down, down...

Fuck. Fuck. Eft's hard, tapered tip was already there, just there, just where Kesst most craved it. And like the ever-obliging gift it was, it was already slick and slippery, already pulsing out more sweet fluid against Kesst's desperately gripping puckered heat. Priming Kesst for this, preparing him, while Kesst just perched there atop it, his head thrown back, his entire body shuddering as he clamped and kissed and felt it, hungry and greedy and brazen.

Eft's groan had deepened into a sustained growl, his wide eyes held to the sight. To how he wasn't yet in at all, to how Kesst was just tasting his slick head like he hadn't the slightest sweet clue how to do this. And suddenly there was the burning, blazing need to show Eft, to prove this to him, he wouldn't regret this, he wouldn't...

So Kesst took a breath, tossed his hair back—and then opened wide, and bore down. Taking that slick, solid length inside him, breath by breath, oh, oh. And Eft was crying out, his entire body curling up on the bed, and the feel of it, inside him, Eft was inside him, opening him, piercing him, splitting him apart—

And Kesst had wanted to take him all the way at once, had wanted to show him that, had needed to flaunt that—but he'd somehow stopped, writhing and shivering all over, hovering up over Eft's also-shuddering body, with Eft stuck halfway up inside him, already everywhere, already way too much. And fuck, this was ridiculous, this was shameful, Kesst couldn't breathe, why couldn't he breathe—

"Hey," Eft croaked, a flare of magic firing into where his hand was still gripped to Kesst's hip—and oh that was too much too, convulsing Kesst even harder, prickling wetness behind his eyes. But his eyes had indeed found Eft's, found them urgent and glimmering on his, as Eft's other shaky hand slipped to Kesst's bare abdomen, and spread wide.

"Let me—help," he choked. "Make—easier."

Oh fuck, oh gods destroy him now, Eft was going to make them fit—and Kesst fervently nodded as he shuddered again, his hand grasping Eft's, pressing it closer. Feeling the magic on both sides, now, flaring itself deep, and finding the place where Eft's pulsing head was driving hard against Kesst's resisting flesh.

Kesst convulsed all over, the shout tearing from his mouth, because oh, oh, there was nothing like this, nothing had ever, ever felt like this. That beautiful swarming magic, that beautiful driving cock, working together now to change him, to remake him. To transform him, so Eft could fill him with his scent and his safety, and Kesst shouted again as he sank a little deeper, his body wildly clutching at the new bit of Eft he'd taken, more, more...

"More," Kesst gasped, helpless, lost. "Take me. Fill me. Remake me so I can fit you. *Please*, Eft."

Eft was desperately nodding, his forehead furrowed with concentration, his magic flaring even harder than before. While Kesst again gasped and shuddered and shouted, his body sinking deeper, deeper, closer...

"More," he begged, his head whipping back and forth, his claws scraping down Eft's front. "More, Eft. *All* of you. *Mine*."

Eft kept nodding, his mouth contorting, the magic flailing up into a torrent of blazing sensation. Driving into Kesst just as hard as his cock, just as overpowering. So close, so close, Kesst could feel it, he was, he was—

There. His trembling arse finally sinking down onto Eft beneath him, with Eft fully buried, embedded, inside him. Deeper than anyone or anything had ever gone, and it felt new, it felt impossible, it felt utterly unreal. It was Kesst forever changed, forever altered, for this.

And he couldn't even move, couldn't even bear to slip a breath away. Needed to just sit there, pinned there, feeling this impossible strength docked so deep inside him. While his invaded body frantically squeezed and convulsed upon it, as if fighting to understand it, to comprehend what this was, how it had possibly remade him like this...

And it was surely learning him too, pulsing and shuddering against Kesst's onslaught, squeezing out its seed inside him. While the magic from Eft's hand kept flickering and searching, as if making even more room, making sure, making him safe...

"All right?" choked Eft's voice, and gods, Kesst could scarcely refocus his eyes, or find Eft's face. But he did, of course he did—and found Eft's cheeks and ears flushed a deep red, his lips parted, his eyes firing with pure, frenzied hunger.

Kesst surely couldn't speak through his groans, but he managed a nod, a tiny little rock of his hips. A movement that somehow shifted his entire belly, all the way up to his navel—and Kesst shouted again as his hands fluttered against it. Against where—he tentatively rocked his hips again—Eft's cockhead was somewhere in the vicinity of his *waist*, oh furious gods above.

"You—great—menace," Kesst moaned, or perhaps wept, as he rocked his hips again, and felt that pole inside him shift and shudder. "You—damned—"

But the words were swarmed, destroyed, at the impossible, unthinkable flare of magic. Magic, rushing up that hard flesh plunged so deep inside him, and unfurling out in a thousand fiery, sparkling streams. Unmaking him, destroying him, blasting away all else until there was—there was—

Kesst's scream rang through his skull, ripping him apart—and his body crumpled, crushed, broke. Clamping writhing and shattering as his seed surged and sprayed, gushing out of him in screeching white torrents, while the euphoria struck and spun and soared—

And then it hitched even higher, as Eft's strength inside him flared, swelled even further, those bollocks tightening between his arse-cheeks, driving that seed up, up, up—and then Eft poured him full. Flooding him from the top down in surge after surge, glutting him with heat and scent and life. Forever changing him, again, remaking him, again, and Kesst could only shout and shudder and drink it up, suck it in, breathe in the scent of it already pooling, already saturating, already new.

Beneath him, Eft had been shouting again too, his body again curled up with almost painful-looking force, his head bent nearly to Kesst's chest. Holding, holding, as Kesst felt him squeezing those last dregs up, giving him all he possibly could, every last drop—

And then, finally, it was done. And Eft sank back down to the bed, his body heavy and sprawling, and painted all over with messy splatters of Kesst's seed. But his hands, his hands were still there on Kesst's waist and hip, his dazed eyes still fixed to the sight, as if he could somehow see deep within, see what he'd done...

Kesst's sweaty hands were clutching there too, his fingers tangling with Eft's, as his breath slowly, shakily exhaled. As Eft's hazy eyes abruptly snapped up to his face, and Kesst could see them fighting to focus, Eft's breath heaving just as hard as his.

"You—" Eft began, his voice breaking—and then he was grasping at Kesst's body, dragging him down to lie atop his sticky chest. And tilting his own hips as Kesst came, putting his knees up, so he didn't even draw all the way out—but oh, the feeling of it moving inside Kesst again, rearranging him, again had him crying out, convulsing into Eft's arms.

"Is it—pain?" Eft's voice gulped, his magic again surging there, seeking with palpable urgency, but Kesst was already shaking his head, burying his face into Eft's chest.

"No pain," he rasped. "Only good. So good. *Fuck.*"

Eft's relief shuddered through them both, his warm arms wrapping tight around Kesst's sweaty back, his fingers spread wide. "So good," he repeated, with a hard, heavy exhale. "Gods, Kesst. You'll be the *death* of me."

He sounded truly stunned, shattered, and it was somehow enough for Kesst to raise his head, to attempt a jab of his finger to Eft's heaving chest. "Me?" he croaked. "You impaled me. Rearranged me. *Remade* me."

And oh, that look on Eft's face, it wasn't regret in the slightest—in truth, it was unnervingly similar to the look on Grimarr's face after they'd killed Skald. Wicked, gleeful triumph, flashing smug and satisfied through his eyes.

And suddenly Kesst was laughing, shrill and uncontrollable, his body shuddering, his head shaking back and forth. "You utter menace," he gulped, between breaths. "You are *never* getting rid of me now, you realize. I am worshipping this cock until I *die*."

Eft laughed too, but again there was relief in it, stuttering deep into his scent. "Good," he whispered. "Just how I want it."

The warmth raced up Kesst's spine, followed by yet another shiver of Eft's magic, seeing it, chasing it. And gods, it was so good, nothing had ever, ever been so good, and Kesst wriggled a little closer, curled up tighter, caught and cradled in Eft's solid embrace, in his safety.

"Do I smell good?" he whispered, into Eft's neck. "More like you?"

In return Eft barked a disbelieving laugh, and clutched Kesst even closer, while his cockhead—which was still tucked inside him—blatantly shuddered. "You smell *exquisite*," Eft breathed. "I mean, you always did, but this—this is—"

His voice broke into another hoarse, incredulous laugh, his warm hands firing hungry little flares into Kesst's skin. "You can... keep it there, right?" Eft whispered now, more tentative than before, or perhaps even ashamed. "For a while?"

But he was speaking to quite possibly the most shameless orc in this mountain, and Kesst pulled up to give him a warm, approving smile. "Of course I can, love, for as long as you like," he murmured. "Want me to marinate a little, do you? Soak in your scent, until it's just as strong as my own?"

Eft's eyes widened with satisfying shock, his throat bobbing as he gasped. While the affection, the sheer blazing fondness, seemed to flare up in Kesst's chest, so strong Eft could surely taste it. But Kesst wanted Eft to taste it, wanted him to know. He was new. This was new. Them.

"And I'll do you one better, love," he whispered. "Why don't we do it all again, and then maybe again. And you can see just how much more you can fit inside me. What that will *smell* like. Will you need to make *more* room, do you think? Make me yours, even more than before?"

And oh, the way Eft groaned, and bucked, and pricked his claws into Kesst's back. His eyes fluttering, his hunger swerving and roaring beneath his fingers, swarming into Kesst's lungs, his soul...

"Gods, yes, Kesst," he breathed, promised. "More. *Mine.*"

20

Kesst couldn't have said how long he and Eft stayed in that bed, writhing and gasping in one another's arms. Learning each other, lavishing each other, remaking each other.

And while it was still Eft making those physical changes, shifting and revising until Kesst could indeed slide all the way down, suck him deep in one smooth, head-spinning stroke, while also holding in multiple loads—along the way, Kesst had somehow decided that he was remaking Eft, too. Taking those lingering uncertainties, those hints of human shame and humiliation, and sweeping them all away with easy, unfettered enthusiasm.

"Of course I want to taste you here," he'd purred at Eft, when Eft had flailed and flushed at the sensation of Kesst's tongue, seeking deep below his bollocks. "Why else do you think the gods gave us such long tongues? *Really*, Eft."

Eft's cheeks had turned fully scarlet by that point, but he'd willingly obliged, and then gasped and writhed with enthralling abandon upon Kesst's onslaught. And when Kesst had lightly suggested that perhaps he could have a turn, Eft had instantly tackled him back, and again proven with dizzying intensity that his tongue could make magic just as well as his cock.

That had, of course, led to a greedy, breathless lesson on Kesst's part, teaching Eft how to suck his first—and hopefully only—prick. And oh, the way it had felt, the way it had looked, Eft's mouth sloppily sucking him while that tongue had done impossible things, would be forever burned into Kesst's memories, together with all the rest.

By the end of it, they were both covered all over with one another's seed, and so exhausted they could barely move. And Kesst found himself again sprawled and sticky on Eft's chest, while Eft's finger gently stroked up and down his wide-open, dripping-wet crease, flaring lazy twinges of magic up inside.

It was the most wonderful feeling, the most sated and content Kesst had surely felt in his life. And it was so easy to finally drift away into sleep, knowing for certain that Eft wanted him, Eft cared for him, Eft trusted him. They'd done this, together.

And that certainty was still there when Kesst's hazy wakefulness slowly returned, a long time later. Because Eft was still here, still lying close and warm beneath him, his hand still possessively gripped against Kesst's bare arse. Even though—Kesst's awareness shifted a little closer—they were no longer alone in the room, and that new scent was instantly familiar. It was Grimarr's scent, now carrying a steady, settled ease in it that Kesst had very nearly forgotten.

"What it means to swear vows to another orc?" Grimarr's distant voice was asking, almost as if repeating a question. "Ach, this is how we make bonds between us. You would swear your sword, your fealty, and your favour. And should the other orc return this with his own pledge, then henceforth, you are mates. And all the Ash-Kai—even my father—shall honour this."

That last bit was said with a grim determination, suggesting that Grimarr would likely still need to throw his weight around on this—but without Ofnir and Skald in the way, that would surely be far easier. And Kesst could feel his own relief reflected in Eft's hollowing chest, in the way his big body relaxed against the bed.

"And the vow is... all it needs?" Eft asked now, his voice unmistakably uncertain. "No jewels, or ceremonies, or the like?"

"No, naught such as that," came Grimarr's reply. "Though I ken most orcs spend a few days mating together, covering one another with their scents. This shall speak their new truth to all our kin, ach? And I ken"—he huffed an amused-sounding laugh—"you have already made a strong start of this."

Eft didn't reply, though his hand had slightly tightened on Kesst's arse. And Kesst could almost feel Grimarr's eyes on it, could taste a familiar wary watchfulness in his scent. "Kesst shall make a good, eager, faithful mate," he said, quiet. "He deserves one who shall treat him with kindness and care in return. One who shall honour him, and keep him safe, and grant him peace."

Kesst could hear Eft swallow, could feel his strong arm drawing him even closer. "I know," Eft said, just as quiet. "I will."

There was another instant's silence, and then an approving-sounding harrumph. "Your payment, then," Grimarr said. "Do you wish it all at once, or in parts? And in coin, or trading-credits?"

Kesst felt himself stiffening, waiting for Eft's answer, for him to change his mind, to take the coin and run—but Eft's arm drew him still closer, and that was surely a twitch of magic, twining into Kesst's skin. "Neither," Eft said, his voice very certain, his familiar stubbornness easing into his scent. "I've decided to stay here indefinitely, and therefore, I want terms from you instead."

Grimarr's surprise was all too obvious in his scent, but he must have waved for Eft to continue, because Eft cleared his throat, and kept speaking. "I want you to swear to me that you'll never allow Kesst to be sent out fighting again, ever. In fact, I want you to swear never to give him another order again. He's done enough. More than enough."

That was surely more surprise in Grimarr's scent, but Eft clearly wasn't done, his voice hardening. "And you're going to make me your Chief Healer," he said, "and let me run my own sickroom as I see fit, without interference. *And*, you're going to move it to somewhere Kesst feels comfortable. Somewhere out of *Ka-esh hell*."

Those were Kesst's words, and he slightly startled at the truth of Eft remembering them, saying them—and that was more of Eft's beautiful magic, sparkling into his skin. "And actually," Eft continued flatly, "you're going to let him choose where it is. You'd pick a good place for us, right, Kesst?"

For us. And Kesst's eyes had snapped open, searching up for Eft's face, and finding him already looking back, his mouth twitching into a slow, affectionate smile. And Kesst felt himself blushing—*blushing!*—as he smiled back, slow and warm and true.

"I'll find us the best place, Eft, of course," he murmured. "Th-thank you."

Good gods, now he was stammering, he'd clearly been reduced to a state of abject lovestruck absurdity—but he truly couldn't find other words, in the midst of the longing and gratefulness and relief. Eft was giving up his payment, the payment he damn well deserved, to keep Kesst away from the war? To find a place he felt *comfortable*?

"And," Eft continued, harder now, his eyes flicking back to

Grimarr, "you're going to give us more warning when you change a damned plan on us. Sending Skald down here on a sudden rampage like that was *ridiculous.*"

Wait. *Grimarr* had sent Skald down for them? That was why Skald had suddenly showed up the way he had, raging and searching for Kesst, with a band of oh-so-helpful witnesses?

But when Kesst twisted to frown up at Grimarr, he didn't look even slightly repentant, shrugging his broad shoulder. "We had no time," he said. "Skald was sure to recall the strength of Kesst's galdr at any breath, and we could not dare show this for what it is. Not whilst my father yet lives."

Not while his father yet lived. It was the most open Grimarr had ever been about this yet, and the most he'd ever admitted about Kesst's gift, too—and Kesst found his disbelief rising as Grimarr continued. "And I yet had other plans in place around this, ach? You ken my father should always have taken this blow with such ease? You ken Skald was not already slower than he ought to have been? And the rest of his orcs, too?"

Wait. *Wait.* Kesst's stilted thoughts were now flicking back, back, to where Kaugir had been very conveniently, very conspicuously, up in the Ash-Kai rooms with his hangers-on, supposedly enjoying an elaborate meal...

"You *drugged* them?" Kesst demanded at him, with genuine rising amusement. "With what? Mushrooms?"

Grimarr's pursed mouth suggested that this was indeed the case, and Kesst felt himself bark a giddy, merry laugh, his head shaking as his eyes met Eft's. "I need to take you on a proper tour of this place," he informed him. "One of Grim's scouts has this whole room full of mushrooms, over in Bautul hell. Which is almost as bad as Ka-esh hell, but not quite. Especially once you've eaten a mushroom or two."

Eft grinned back at him, his eyes dancing with warmth, his hand flaring more sparks of heat into Kesst's skin. "I'd love a proper tour with you," he said softly, tugging Kesst's bared, sticky body a little closer—but then frowning as he glanced back up toward Grimarr again. "Is there anything else you need, then? Are we settled?"

Grimarr huffed a wry laugh, clearly knowing when he was dismissed, and he brought his fist to his chest, briefly bowing toward them both. "Ach, we are settled, Chief Healer," he said. "I thank you both for your great help in this, my brothers."

Kesst felt his face and ears heating, his hand quickly waving it away, while against him Eft snorted, and shook his head. "You can thank us by dealing with your foul father next," he replied flatly. "And by leaving us the hell alone for a few days. No new raids, no bloody obnoxious orcs I need to keep awake, *nothing*."

To Kesst's relief, Grimarr was clever enough not to argue with this, and finally took his leave. And Kesst found himself swallowing hard as he met Eft's eyes, searched his face, inhaled his stunning scent, now with all those new shades of *him* embedded so deep within it.

"You really—didn't," Kesst stammered, "need to do that. That payment—that was yours. You should have still—taken the coin. Not wasted it on—on *me*."

But the stubbornness was already here, flooding Eft's scent with strength and purpose. "Not wasted," he said firmly. "You deserve some freedom from all this mess. Some peace. Maybe some time to come to terms with it all, too."

Kesst's head was shaking, his lips pressing tightly together, his eyes already prickling with heat. "I don't deserve any of that, Eft," he croaked. "I don't. I was still complicit. I *was* a greedy, ruined—"

But Eft's head was shaking too, and his fingers came up to brush a twitch of magic into Kesst's lips. "No," he said, so certain. "You don't talk about my mate that way. You're *fallegur*, Kesst. *Stórglæsilegur*. Quick. Clever. Brave. Generous. The most innocent orc in this mountain. *Ég elska þig.*"

Kesst's breath had hitched, his eyes widening on Eft's face. Had he really, really just called him his *mate*, surely he hadn't meant that, hadn't meant that entire earlier conversation with Grimarr either, because—

Eft had clearly caught himself, grimacing, and Kesst could feel him drawing in a deep breath. "I mean," he continued, his voice lowering, "if you would welcome it, Kesst, I—I would be truly honoured to call you my mate. But you might want more time to consider it, with all you've been through, and I'm more than happy to wait, until whenever you're—"

But Kesst's body was already shivering, flailing up, his own hand fluttering to cover Eft's mouth. "Yes," he gulped. "Yes, Eft, gods yes. But you might regret it, you might finally realize what a high-maintenance disaster I am, you will never get rid of me, and I—I—"

And he was weeping, damn it, full-on weeping, the sobs escaping in thick ugly gasps. Eft wanted to make him his mate, he couldn't truly want that, now surely he would change his mind, he had to...

"Good," came Eft's reply, sounding rather choked too—and when Kesst desperately focused his wet eyes on Eft again, he was fervently nodding, his big warm hands stroking up Kesst's heaving chest, until they found his face. Cradling it, as if he were something prized, something precious.

"Good," Eft said again, his bright eyes fixed on Kesst's. "Then I want to swear a vow to you, Kesst of Clan Ash-Kai. I swear to give you my fealty, and my favour, and my protection, and whatever the hell else you want from me. Anything you want."

Anything you want. Those were again Kesst's words, and now Eft was here just saying them, swearing them, vowing them. Like it was nothing, everything, like he really, really wanted this, he couldn't really want this, but he'd said it, how had he just said it? Said that, to *Kesst*?

Kesst couldn't stop staring, and weeping, and wildly shaking his head against Eft's still-cradling hands—but Eft, the stubborn menace, hadn't even slightly faltered, his eyes watching, his lip jutting out. Waiting. Waiting.

He wanted Kesst—to say it. To swear it. Finish it. And Kesst couldn't, he couldn't, he—

"Then I pledge you my troth, Efterar of Clan Ash-Kai," his voice whispered. "I grant you my favour, and my sword, and my fealty. I shall keep you safe, and fed, and filled, so long as I am able, and so long as you shall wish."

It was the traditional Ash-Kai pledge, the one he'd known all his life, the one he'd woven into so many of his tales. And now he'd said it, he'd truly, truly said it, and he'd meant it. And Eft was staring back at him, staring like he'd been stunned, like it was the most powerful tale Kesst had ever told. And maybe it was, it was, his magic surging and soaring, pouring out his heart.

"And the mortal basked and worshipped at the angel's feet, for all the rest of his days," he breathed. "Where beneath the angel's many blessings, he grew fat and content and whole again. And in return for the angel's benevolent healing, the mortal offered him all the earthly delights he could afford. Good meat, and rest, and comfort, and pleasures beyond his wildest imaginings. And together, they built a new home, and found great peace."

The words rang and spun between them, hovering with astonishing strength, holding them both rapt within it. And there wasn't even room to wonder if it had all been pure selfish indulgence, because Kesst believed it, he believed it so deeply he was fully lost in it, lost in Eft's shifting, beautiful eyes. In the way Eft's magic suddenly swerved to life, and flooded back into the full length of him. Surging and soaring into Kesst's skin, into his flesh, into his heart and his bones. Remaking him in this, from this, from the ashes of his sins. Mating him. Healing him.

And when Eft's shaking arms finally pulled Kesst close, pulled him beneath, and once again filled him with that last missing piece, Kesst knew it for certain, forever changed.

He was innocent, and he was whole.

EPILOGUE

I f Kesst had ever imagined that a new sickroom would improve the attitudes of Orc Mountain's injured inhabitants, he'd clearly been downright deranged.

"If you say *one more word* to my brilliant mate," he hissed at Silfast's hideous howling face, "who is, incidentally, probably about to save your sorry life, I will personally claw out your eyeballs while you sleep. So *fuck. Off.*"

Miraculously, that actually shut Silfast up, and he sagged backwards onto the bed behind him, protectively squeezing his eyes shut. While beside Kesst, Eft sent a grateful flare of magic into his arm, and then reached forward, settling his hand against Silfast's head. And beneath him, Silfast slowly relaxed, the visible pain leaving his face, his eyes fluttering as he exhaled.

Kesst watched it all with genuine appreciation, his hand stroking up and down Eft's back. Because even after spending multiple moons witnessing Eft's astonishing skill, he'd never yet tired of seeing it. Of tasting that magic, feeling it take whatever misery and pain stood before it, and changing it. Remaking it. Making it whole again.

"Brilliant, Eft," he murmured, easing a little closer, inhaling his familiar, glorious scent. "As always."

Eft shot him a brief, rueful look, another affectionate twinge of magic, before flipping his attention back to Silfast again. But Kesst just kept standing there for another long moment, silently marvelling at his spectacular mate, and the new life they'd somehow made together. This new home.

Part of that, of course, was their clean, spacious new sickroom. It was no longer situated down in stuffy Ka-esh hell, but instead—as Eft had promised—Kesst had chosen a new place, a place where he felt comfortable. A project that had resulted in Kesst spending multiple days stalking about the mountain, and sniffing at various rooms—but finally he'd decided on a large, open room at the very heart of the mountain. A room well away from the Ash-Kai summit where Kaugir still desperately clung to his rule, and also well away from Ka-esh hell, where Kesst's mother had grieved. And instead, it was a plain, straightforward, bland-scented room, featuring excellent ventilation, an adjoining latrine, and a cozy fireplace—all assets that would suit not only Kesst, but Eft's patients, too.

"It's perfect," Eft had firmly told Kesst that first night, once Kesst had brought him there, and tentatively explained the room's various qualities. "I knew you'd find the best place for us. Thank you."

Kesst had attempted to wave it away, and to remind Eft that it was *his* sickroom, not theirs—but predictably, Eft had refused to hear it, and had instead begun a veritable campaign of making love to Kesst in multiple locations throughout the room, filling it with their scents. And once that had been established, he'd helped Kesst scrub the room, and they'd brought up the beds, and picked the best one together, and covered it with their scents, too. And after all that, Kesst had had to admit that the room really did feel like his now, just as much as it felt like Eft's. It felt like... *theirs*.

"Efterar!" shouted a voice behind them. "Olarr has been wounded scouting, again!"

Both Kesst and Eft spun around at once, frowning toward where two Bautul orcs were dragging in a very bloody Olarr. And as usual, Kesst stalked over to investigate, directing the orcs to leave Olarr's ruined clothes at the door, and then escorting Olarr to the nearest unoccupied bed, and promising that Eft would see him shortly.

Of course, that was only the beginning of the day's events, and Kesst soon found himself caught up in the rhythm and flow of life in their sickroom. Not only assessing and directing any new arrivals, but also keeping an eye on their patients' sleep and pain levels, helping them to the latrine, handing out water, and just doing whatever else Eft needed. While also keeping up a steady stream of cheerful commentary and gossip, something he'd only done at first to entertain Eft—but he'd since discovered that it made his own days far more entertaining, too. And it had turned out that sickroom gossip was by far the best gossip, and Kesst had somehow gained a reputation as someone to seek out, whenever there was important information to learn or share. Or, even better, whenever there were secret romantic entanglements to discover.

"Wounded by that same plucky human yet again, hmmm?" he asked a pained-looking Olarr, once Eft had finished staunching the worst of his wounds. "So *odd*, that a great powerful warrior like you hasn't managed to put that one in his place yet. Although"—Kesst thoughtfully tapped his chin—"I heard the other day that your little nemesis smells very similar to a certain well-known Preian *general*?"

Olarr's blood-streaked face turned a highly betraying shade of pink, his mouth frowning as it opened and closed. "I am not—" he began, and then winced, narrowing his eyes toward Kesst with obvious suspicion. "Ach, has Grimarr put you up to this?"

Grimarr had, in fact, been pointedly hinting about Olarr's mysterious human last time he'd stopped by looking for news—something he now did multiple times each week—and Kesst gave his most enigmatic smile, tossing his hair over his shoulder. "It's our Ash-Kai duty," he coolly informed Olarr. "However, it's also *your* duty to not drag Preia's whole army here for Grim to deal with, just because *you* can't control yourself around a pretty piece of arse with a sword."

Olarr winced again, wiping his big hand at his bloody face. "I have not lost *control*," he said, his voice firm. "And he shall not betray us to his kin. I am sure of this. He is too..."

"Too addicted to having your prick in that pretty arse, after he's put you on your knees?" Kesst supplied over his shoulder as he went to fill a waterskin, swaying his own pretty arse in its tight trousers as he went. "Perfectly understandable, of course. I'll let Grim know, and he'll likely let it go. As long as *you*"—he jabbed a claw toward Olarr as he brought back the waterskin— "make sure you keep your feisty little man *very* happy and quiet, hmmm?"

Olarr gave an irritable-sounding grunt, but that was surely relief in his eyes, too, and he didn't seem inclined to argue. Thankfully, because there was a rising commotion across the room, and Kesst whipped around to the aggravating sight and scent of Ulfarr, who was currently wildly staggering against Eft, while also spouting a veritable fountain of blood from his horribly broken arm.

"You have near killed me, you craven sneaking bewitcher!" Ulfarr was hollering, his face mottled with sweat and pain, his broken arm spraying blood across Eft's previously clean tunic. "If you ken I shall not tell my father and all my Skai brothers about this, you—"

Thankfully he broke off there, his eyes rolling back, his big body crashing down onto the bed behind him. While Eft— who had obviously just knocked him out—roughly grasped

Ulfarr's broken arm again, and yanked it straight with vicious, painful-looking force. An action that should have perhaps lessened the taste of Eft's rising anger, but Kesst could feel it swinging higher, surging dark and bitter through the air.

Kesst grimaced and swiftly strode over toward Eft, while silently cursing Ulfarr and all his foul Skai clan. Their ongoing aggression and ungratefulness toward Eft had become one of the greatest irritations in Kesst's otherwise delightful new life, and had indeed seemed to worsen over time. Partly due to Kaugir's continued public disdain of his son's "craven pet bewitcher", Kesst knew—but also, without question, because of him. Because he'd once been ostensibly available for those bastards' pleasure, and now was most decidedly not. A fact which had taken these vermin some time to fully appreciate, and which they'd since returned with a tedious onslaught of threats, mockery, and derision.

"Deep breaths, Eft," Kesst said now, from where he was slipping up behind him, and sliding his arms around his waist. "Gods, these Skai are obnoxious ungrateful louts, aren't they? Can't you just let him bleed out for a while?"

He could feel Eft slightly relaxing under his touch, his anger slowly pooling away, even as he gave an irritable shake of his head. "Not yet," he grunted, as his magic shifted and reoriented itself, his hand now settling against Ulfarr's face. "He's got a head wound, too. Lucky he's not dead."

Kesst exhaled into Eft's neck, giving a wry smile as he shook his head. "Unlucky, you mean," he murmured. "You're far too good for us, Eft. A mere mortal would have happily let this reeking cretin croak long ago."

But Eft would never do that, Kesst knew very well, even when the orc desperately deserved it—and he leaned in closer, gently sliding his hand up beneath Eft's tunic, and scraping his long sharp claws against his torso, just the way Eft liked best. And in return, he could feel Eft relaxing a little more, the magic flowing faster and stronger into Ulfarr beneath him, working miracles with its usual breathtaking ease.

So Kesst just stayed there, touching and caressing his brilliant generous mate, pressing the occasional kiss into the back of his neck. Knowing, now, in a way he hadn't before, that Eft's anger would still be lurking there deep within, a constant quiet struggle in his outwardly stolid existence—and that left to his own devices, he would keep burying it ever deeper, drowning it in work and hunger and exhaustion. And as much as the vile subjects of Eft's rage deserved it, Eft certainly didn't deserve to be stuck in that miserable cycle, either—so Kesst had begun doing everything within his power to head it off before it began. Food and jokes and gossip always helped, but the most consistently effective means he'd found yet were his own devoted affections—and the more blatant, the better.

"He's got to be almost stable now, right, love?" he murmured now, scraping his claws just a little harder against Eft's chest, letting his teeth drag lightly against his neck. "How about a quick suck, then? I'm running *very* low on you right now, you must know."

That was another intriguing new truth he'd learned these past moons—just how much Eft loved Kesst walking around with copious amounts of his own fresh seed inside him. A healer quirk, most certainly, what with Eft being able to feel that seed hidden inside Kesst with every touch and breath. And of course, Kesst was more than willing to oblige Eft in such a devious decadence, another secret indulgence shared just between them—and he'd indeed grown so accustomed to it that he found himself becoming rather sulky and snappy whenever he was deprived.

"Oh, come on, Eft," he whined into his shoulder, feeling Eft's magic working harder, faster, finishing up whatever he was doing. "Want to taste you. Want to fill my empty belly with you until I can't possibly *hold* any more."

Eft huffed a hoarse, deeply satisfying moan, his magic working even more frantically than before—and then it whipped entirely away from Ulfarr, and back toward Kesst, where it belonged. And Kesst purred his eager approval as he yanked Eft close, briefly slipping his tongue into his succulent mouth, revelling in the feel of Eft's big hands hungrily caressing his bare chest—and then smoothly, swiftly making his way downwards, kissing and licking and nipping as he went, holding Eft's hazy gaze.

And oh, Eft was looking, he loved looking, loved seeing his greedy mate lavishing him, worshipping him with shameless abandon. It was another one of those things Kesst had learned, that the more brazen he was, the more Eft liked it—as long as Kesst's attentions were fully focused toward him, of course. Which of course they always were—Kesst's own possessive jealousy of Eft's attentions truly knew no bounds, and he was deeply gratified that Eft felt the same—but what was the harm in drawing a few hungry eyes while they revelled in one another? Why not flaunt Kesst's flagrant, voracious hunger for his gorgeous mate, and reinforce Eft's clear superiority over all the other useless blockheads in this mountain?

And indeed, Kesst could already feel several eyes on them, several hungry scents from the beds around the room— Abjorn, for certain, and Olarr too—but Kesst kept his own eyes firmly on Eft's as he slithered fully to his knees on the floor, and deftly pulled Eft's cock out of his trousers. Taking a brief, dizzy instant to breathe it in, to lust after its stunning beauty, to smell his own scent all over it. Only his scent, only ever his own scent, and oh, he would never stop worshipping Eft for that, ever.

So he started by just sipping at it, reverently kissing at that smooth silken crown, tasting the soft pulses of seed Eft was already giving him. Already rewarding him, like he always did, and Kesst moaned as he slid his hungry hands up Eft's thighs, and sucked that head deeper into his mouth. Feeling it throb and flare at the contact, shuddering out more rich sweetness onto Kesst's swirling, seeking tongue.

Eft had moaned too, his hips reflexively bucking, his eyes firmly on Kesst's face—he never looked away, no matter how large or rapt their audience—and Kesst smiled around that beauty in his mouth as he sucked it deeper. Halfway now, halfway was easy these days, and he moaned again as Eft pumped out even more hot seed for him, sliding it down his throat. Easing the way, wanting to go deeper, so Kesst willingly did that too, letting that slick head nudge and seek against the convulsing tightness of his throat. Delving further, further, and Kesst breathed hard through his nose as he caressed Eft's thighs and arse and bollocks, willed himself to relax, to open, to let that driving heft fill his hungry throat...

Eft's expression was now something between agony, awe, and ecstasy, his shaky hand slipping down, settling against Kesst's neck. Wanting to make it easy, Kesst knew, wanting to make them fit without pain or discomfort, like he'd done with Kesst's arse—but they'd already been over this multiple times, and with effort, Kesst narrowed his watering eyes up toward Eft's face, and made a valiant attempt at an open-mouthed pout. He was going to do this himself, he needed to earn this himself, and he accordingly felt Eft's hand drop again, even as he hissed a heated, frustrated groan. Wanting more, but not more, his scent heavy and rich with his longing, his craving, his thwarted, desperate hunger.

And Kesst was damn well giving his magnificent mate more, he was angling his head, sinking him even deeper down his throat. His teeth scraping, now, his tongue trapped and useless, but oh, the look in Eft's watching eyes, the wonder, the way his shaky hands were now caressing Kesst's reddened, sweaty face. Shuddering little twinges of magic as they went, so careful and gentle, his eyes rapt and reverent, as if the sight of

Kesst on his knees with a pole down his throat was the most perfect thing he'd ever seen in his life.

Because it was, of course it was, and Kesst helplessly groaned as he sucked even deeper. His throat wildly protesting and convulsing at the powerful flesh now firmly opening it, filling it, conquering it. Demanding Kesst's worship, demanding even more, and oh, he would give more, even if the water had begun streaking down his cheeks, even if Eft's throbbing strength was now touching places no other being had ever touched before. It was Kesst's, and his alone, and he had it and he was taking it, he was sucking it all the way down, his lips were kissing at Eft's groin, fuck, fuck, *fuck*—

Eft shouted and sprayed without warning, that cock in Kesst's mouth shuddering from base to tip, surging it out in pulse after furious pulse. Emptying it straight down Kesst's gullet, deep into his greedy empty belly. And if Kesst could have screamed he would have, because now he was yanking down his trousers and pouring out too, his own ecstasy trammelling everything else as it swept and soared. Strong enough that he found himself choking, his breath entirely gone, his lungs heaving for air—and thankfully Eft wrenched himself out, just in time. His hand now circling against Kesst's throat, soothing it, even as they both kept groaning and trembling with the sheer shouting euphoria, blazing back and forth between them.

But then, slowly, it settled again. Settled quiet and soft, with Eft still blinking down at Kesst with abject awe in his dazed eyes, while Kesst gave back a slow, deeply satisfied smile.

"Told you I'd take you all the way eventually, love," he purred, licking at his swollen wet lips, and leisurely rubbing a hand at his bare belly. "Mmmm, that's so much better. Although"—he felt his ears faintly flushing as he glanced downwards—"I *might* have made a *slight* mess of your boots. Again."

But Eft was still blankly staring at him, still with that highly satisfying reverence in his eyes. "Fuck," he breathed, the word a single hard exhale. "Fuck my boots. Gods damn it, Kesst. *Þú ert svo fallegur. Svo stórglæsilegur.*"

And Kesst kept smiling, feeling it pull even wider, feeling the affection spark and shimmer in his eyes. "Aren't I, though?" he murmured. "But only for you, Eft. All yours."

Eft groaned again, his eyes squeezing shut, and he dragged Kesst back to his feet again, dragged him bodily up into his arms. And then he carried him over to the nearby workbench, propping Kesst upon it, so he could lean in, and ravish his mouth with his hungry tongue and teeth. "Gods," he breathed, between kisses. "How am I this lucky. I cannot be this lucky. *Fuck.*"

Kesst laughed and moaned and shivered as he kissed him back, twining his arms and legs tight around Eft's powerful body. "Not lucky," he breathed. "Just stuck with me, and with all my—"

But Eft nipped at his lip, pressed him a sharp flare of magic, and Kesst shivered again as he leaned closer, and clung to Eft with all his strength. Because Eft had to know he was stuck, he had to know all Kesst's grievous faults by now. Not only did Kesst still require excessive amounts of attention and reassurance, but he'd also begun having the most hellish dreams, waking up sweating and writhing to sickening visions of Ofnir and Skald returned to life again. The feeling so real, and so horrifying, that he'd once even vomited into their bed—but Eft had never faltered, had always been there with his touch and his healing, his fervent, familiar voice.

I'm here. You're safe. They will never, ever touch you again.

But even Eft hadn't been able to take away those scents on Kesst's skin, not only of Skald and Ofnir, but of every other orc Kesst had ever touched, too. Several of them absolute pricks like Ulfarr, orcs who continued to barge around giving Eft incessant grief, even as he was still obliged to touch and smell and heal them. And while Eft insisted that he didn't care about smelling their scents on Kesst, Kesst had found that he himself increasingly did—to the point where he'd once asked, quiet and shameful, if Eft could somehow peel away his skin, and still keep him alive.

And bless Eft, because he hadn't betrayed a trace of mockery or disbelief, but had instead yanked Kesst close, flooded him with magic, and told him he smelled beautiful as he was. That he was the most beautiful person in the world. That he could drown in the perfection of his scent.

"Love you, Kesst," he was whispering now, his forehead resting against Kesst's, his hands swarming flutters of magic into his back. "*Ég elska þig. Fullkomni sálufélaginn minn.*"

My perfect mate, it meant, it was Aelakesh Eft had learned all on his own, and Kesst laughed as he shook his head, and drew Eft closer. Squeezing so hard it hurt, but Eft only squeezed back, so close, so safe. Changing him again, remaking him again, like he'd done so, so many times.

"*Ég elska þig líka*," Kesst mumbled, into Eft's shoulder. "*Svo mikið, eins og þú veist.*"

I love you too, it meant. *So much, you know.*

"Ach, I know," Eft whispered, so soft. "*Mine.*"

His. It sent the usual furious shiver up Kesst's back, even as he felt himself pulling away a little, and flashing a teasing grin up at Eft's face. "Did you just say *ach*?" he demanded. "Good gods, Eft, this mountain is finally getting to you. Soon I'll find you off licking at bloody axe-blades, and raiding innocent townspeople's cellars."

Eft gave a choked-sounding chuckle, another nip at Kesst's mouth, even as his eyes briefly darted toward their still-attentive audience. Knowing very well that saying such things was still risky, as long as Kaugir remained in power, with all his devoted Skai and Ash-Kai minions—but Kesst had the ultimate faith in Grimarr's ongoing plots, and in the ever-tightening web he kept weaving around his father. A web Kesst was firmly committed to supporting, not only with his information, but also with casual words and jokes and laughter, and even the occasional tale, too. Something for these wounded blockheads to ponder while they lay here, while Grimarr's own brilliant Chief Healer saved their sorry lives.

It was something Kesst had even taken willingly on the road these past moons, to the fringes of those raids and battles against the humans. He still didn't love travelling, but it was so much better—and safer—with Eft there, by his side, in his arms at nights. And Eft being there on Grimarr's raids also meant that Grimarr's raids were the most successful, with the fewest casualties and cruelties. All of which, Kesst very well knew, was just another part of making Grimarr captain of a united Orc Mountain, sooner rather than later.

And once that happened, Kesst was quite possibly never leaving the mountain again. He was going to stay here in his cozy sickroom with his spectacular mate, and enjoy his well-earned reputation as the mountain's cleverest, most eloquent, most unattainable prize. Who now also undoubtedly possessed—Kesst gave Eft another smug smile—the mountain's deepest throat, too.

"So lucky," Eft murmured, his eyes already gone rather hazy again, his warm hand rising to caress gently, reverently, against Kesst's neck. "So perfect."

And oh, it would never get old, ever, and Kesst felt himself preening beneath it, tossing his hair over his shoulder, flashing Eft his best, brightest smile. "If you're trying to get that delicious pole down my throat again, love," he purred, "you know you only ever need to ask."

But Eft never truly needed to ask, not with that warmth shimmering in his eyes, in his touch. Not with his healing and his loyalty, his stubbornness and his safety. His remaking, and how in it, he'd somehow also allowed Kesst to remake himself, too.

So Kesst caught Eft's rising question with a hard, desperate kiss, pouring out all his affection and gratefulness and hope. And then he gracefully sank to his knees, and drank his saviour deep.

THE END

BONUS SCENE

After three full days of mating, Kesst should have been sore, starving, and utterly spent, without a drop of seed left to spill.

But—Kesst flipped up on top of Eft's naked, sticky body again, and flashed him his best smile—his brilliant new mate was a healer. And one of the many mind-blowing things he'd discovered these past days was that Eft's healing couldn't only deal with blood and pain, but also with tedious obstacles like hunger, and soreness, and empty bollocks. And that as long as Eft had a few good hours' sleep—and no other orcs to heal— he could keep them both going for multiple rounds on end, spilling so many loads between them that Kesst had entirely lost count.

"Ready for another go, then, love?" Kesst purred, running his hands down Eft's sticky, bulky chest, revelling in how even that brought up a fresh waft of their combined scents. A beautiful blend that grew stronger every time they finished, and— Kesst leaned closer, inhaling deep—would surely never fade, after this.

"Whatever you want," Eft replied, his dazed eyes sweeping

with awed, worshipful reverence up and down Kesst's bared, seed-splattered body, and now lingering on his swollen, leaking cock. "Anything you want."

It was again Kesst's line, one Eft had repeatedly thrown out these past days, to the point where it had begun feeling less like Kesst's, and more like theirs. Like another growing bond between them, another prayer in their deepening worship of one another.

And Kesst had found it surprising, and also deeply satisfying, to realize that Eft truly did want to worship him, too. That he honestly seemed to think Kesst was the most beautiful, most alluring, most delightful person he'd ever met in his life. A sentiment that had led to astonishing rounds of conversation and laughter in between bouts of lovemaking, and to Eft constantly touching him, kissing him, flaring magic inside him. And Eft just looking at him like this, like he'd never witnessed anything so engrossing as Kesst dropping a hand to his own swollen prick, and slowly, smoothly stroking up its full length. A shameless, self-indulgent display that instantly had Eft groaning, his eyes fluttering, his tooth biting his lip.

"You like that, love?" Kesst murmured, as he again stroked up, even slower than before. Watching Eft watch him, with such gratifying wonder in his dazed eyes. "You like looking at your mate's hungry prick? Like seeing me touch it for you?"

Eft fervently nodded, groaning again as he watched, so Kesst slowed his strokes further, even as he increased the pressure. Bringing up a good dollop of fresh white seed, and then catching it on his fingers before stroking back down again.

"So perfect," Eft finally croaked, his hazy eyes flicking up to Kesst's before dropping again. "So beautiful, Kesst."

Kesst couldn't help preening a little at the praise, and he of course kept stroking, squeezing out more, slicking himself to a glossy, sweet-scented shine. Finding himself oddly savouring the chance to do this, to show off his cock for a lover, and have said lover keep staring like this, without even a trace of jealousy or shame in his scent. Because Kesst did have quite a nice cock, he well knew, with excellent length and girth and responsiveness, and a tendency to spray its seed with considerable force and distance. All desirable attributes that orcs like Skald had always preferred to firmly ignore, in favour of focusing solely on Kesst's arse and his mouth.

But Eft just kept staring, his tongue brushing against his lips, his groan now a low, steady growl in his throat. Even as his eyes very briefly darted to Kesst's again, the flush on his face deepening, while a telltale twitch skittered through his scent. As if he wanted to say something, but wasn't sure how.

"What is it, love?" Kesst asked, pausing his stroking to bring his seed-slick fingers to Eft's mouth, just because he could. "Would you like something else?"

He'd continued to learn these past days that despite the depths of Eft's hunger, he often needed prompting to speak it, to break through that lingering uncertainty and shame. And he could indeed see Eft swallowing, dragging in breath, as his tongue willingly curled out against Kesst's fingers.

"Have you," he began, and then again licked at Kesst's fingers, almost as if drawing courage. "You have... taken another orc before. Right? I mean, I can smell it, so..."

Kesst blinked down at Eft, and found that he'd frozen to shocked, speechless stillness, for the first time in days. Eft wanted to know if Kesst had taken another orc. If he'd done the fucking, he meant. And why did he want to know that, what did he want to hear, what kind of answer wouldn't upset him, and...

"Hey," Eft said, his eyes suddenly far clearer than before, his hand catching Kesst's in his. "You don't have to answer, all right? It's not important. Doesn't mean anything."

Oh. Kesst felt his shoulders sagging, his mouth twitching into a wan little smile, while something kicked and squirmed in his belly. Gods, Eft had been so, so generous toward him, so impossibly kind and patient, and Kesst wanted to return that with honesty. Wanted to trust him. To try.

"Right, well," he made himself reply, his voice thick, his eyes not quite meeting Eft's. "I have. Done that, I mean. But I certainly wouldn't expect anything like that from you, and I definitely don't want you to see me differently because of it either, I know a lot of orcs don't like—"

But Eft had suddenly jerked up to sitting beneath Kesst, bringing their faces close. And his expression was genuinely confused, the truth of that echoed by the bewilderment in his scent, the uncertain tilt of his head. "Why would I see you differently because of that?" he asked. "I thought orcs weren't supposed to care about such things?"

Kesst grimaced and vaguely flapped his hands, not wanting to get into the unpleasant truth that some orcs very much did—especially the ones like Skald and Ofnir, who always considered you the... *recipient* in the encounter. And once Kesst had gained a reputation as such, it had become even more unlikely, if not impossible, to find an orc willing to welcome that from him, let alone to walk around reeking of his fresh scent.

It meant Kesst had really only done the fucking a handful of times, despite his vast experience—and he could still remember every single one. Could remember how damned good it had felt, how surreal, how powerful. Burying himself deep in hot hungry flesh, spraying out his seed into it, tasting his scent slowly seeping through his lover's skin...

"So... you liked it?" Eft asked, tentative now, as more uncertainty twitched through his scent. "Or not?"

Kesst grimaced again, but Eft was still waiting, and Kesst could taste a trace of his rising stubbornness, too. Truly wanting to know this, and he'd said he didn't care, gods please let him not care—

"I liked it," Kesst managed, far too quickly. "But again, I

wouldn't expect you to ever want that from me. You know I still *love* your cock, and I will happily get on my knees and suck it inside me at every possible—"

But suddenly Eft's warm fingers were here, covering Kesst's mouth, breaking off his voice. "So would you," he whispered, "ever consider doing that... with me?"

With him. With *him*?

Kesst's mouth had fallen open against Eft's hand, his thoughts flailing in a dozen directions at once, while he stared blankly at Eft's earnest eyes. An earnestness that was also there in his scent, was he really asking this, he could not be really asking this? With *him*?

"Um," Kesst gulped, as a sharp, sustained shiver wrenched up his spine. "You wouldn't really *want*—"

But Eft pressed him a flare of magic this time, hard enough to slightly sting his lips. "I would," he said, "like to try it with you, Kesst. If *you* would like it."

Kesst heard himself whimper against Eft's hand, the sound strained and helpless, as another forceful shiver rippled up his back. "You wouldn't," he tried again. "You can't, Eft. You've never even—"

And good gods, Eft was asking Kesst to be his first, maybe his only, to put his cock and his seed *inside* him—and Kesst whimpered again as Eft pressed him another flare of magic, softer this time. "I want to," Eft insisted, and oh, that stubbornness was there again, all over his eyes, his touch, his scent. "Now, what's the easiest way. On my knees?"

This could not be happening, Eft could not truly be offering this, he *couldn't*—but when Kesst somehow nodded, shaky and stunned, Eft promptly slid out from beneath him, and turned over onto his hands and knees. Giving Kesst a sudden, shocking invitation that he'd never once imagined receiving in his life, and for a moment he could only stare and wonder, while his heart suddenly began fighting to pound out of his chest. This was not happening. This was *not happening...*

He could see Eft quivering, could taste a flicker of his uncertainty, oh gods was he going to take it back—but then Eft purposefully glanced over his shoulder, and loudly cleared his throat. "Is there—something else I should do first?" he asked. "Some way I should ready myself, or—"

And curse him, not only was Kesst being the worst, *worst* mess over this, but he was being a terrible lover besides. And far too late, he hurriedly shifted up to his shaky knees behind Eft, and caressed both hands down that broad, slightly trembling back.

"Nothing else you need to do, love," he gulped, as he drank up the sight of Eft like this, the feel of him, the sheer perfection of him. "Nothing at all. This is perfect."

He could feel Eft's breath exhaling, his big body relaxing beneath his touch, so Kesst kept stroking, and lowered his mouth to Eft's back. "Perfect," he whispered again, pressing a soft, gentle kiss against the warm skin. "And maybe you'll let me touch you and taste you first, to make it easier for you? And you'll tell me if you change your mind, or—"

"I won't," came Eft's reply, husky but hard—but then he huffed a laugh, and shook his head. "I mean, I'll tell you if I do, but—I won't, Kesst. I want to. Try this with you."

Kesst could feel Eft's effort in saying it, in being the one to be brazen and shameless, in the face of Kesst's total ineptness. When *Eft* was the one who'd never done this before, and suddenly the affection was crashing over Kesst, crushing him, and he couldn't help slipping his arms around Eft's torso, and squeezing as tightly as he could.

"I'm so honoured," he whispered. "Thank you, Eft."

Eft huffed an unsteady-sounding laugh, and shook his head. "Should be me thanking you," he breathed. "Now show me how it's done, will you? Trying to be patient, here."

Kesst heard himself laugh too, hoarse and disbelieving, but somehow discovered that he could move again, think again. And as he began stroking Eft's back again, kissing him again, he found himself suddenly drowning in the determination to make this as good as he possibly could. If Eft was truly giving him this, making Kesst his first, he was damn well going to remember it, because it was going to be *spectacular*.

So Kesst refocused his efforts on caressing as he kissed, working with steady pressure on the big muscles of Eft's back, easing away the remaining tension in his kneeling form. While also slowly moving downwards, gently kissing and tonguing toward Eft's firm, beautifully rounded arse. Taking his good time, making sure it was all pleasure, making sure Eft stayed pliant and receptive under his touch.

His first gentle lick at the top of Eft's crease set him tensing up again, but Kesst kept working, kept stroking, until Eft gradually relaxed again. And then he eased down more, more, keeping it careful and predictable, until he found that sweet pucker of heat.

Eft's heavy breaths had instantly lowered to a growl, his body tightening against Kesst's tongue—but they'd already done this several times now, and Kesst kept caressing, licking, lingering, until Eft slowly opened beneath his touch. Letting his tongue delve just slightly inside, and Kesst purred his low satisfaction as he gave Eft more, opened him more, felt him shudder and sway under his kiss.

"Still good?" he murmured at Eft, between gentle plunges of his tongue, and Eft's nod was thankfully instantaneous, his back even arching a little more. So Kesst kept licking, and soon slipped a finger over, too. Slowly, gently nudging it, delving into that hot silken clutch, feeling Eft grip and grasp at him, oh gods, *oh*.

"Good," Kesst breathed, between licks, as he gradually

began working a second finger in alongside the first. "So good, Eft. So gorgeous, with me inside you like this."

Eft's growl hitched into a harsh grunt, his head twitching a fervent nod, and Kesst smiled as he kept licking, slipping his fingers deeper into that tantalizing heat. "Feels so good, love," he purred. "Looks so good. Love tasting you. Love feeling inside you."

Eft grunted again, his body now pressing back a little into Kesst's touch, clearly wanting more—so of course Kesst gave more, sinking his fingers even deeper, marvelling at how Eft clamped and convulsed against them. Wanting them there. Wanting him. *Him.*

"Want you," Eft breathed, in a stunning echo of Kesst's own thoughts. "Rest of you. *Now.*"

And now it was Kesst growling, his already-overwhelmed cock throbbing and bobbing at his groin. "You sure?" he asked, even as he was already drawing his fingers out, and pressing another long, tongue-heavy kiss to that softened, opened heat. "Now?"

Eft jerked a nod, and even pressed back toward Kesst, opening up more. Being blatantly shameless about this, for him—and Kesst felt himself blinking hard as he gave one last, languid kiss, and then drew away. Taking a strange, dangling moment to drink up what he'd done, at the sight of Eft so relaxed and ready for him, *presenting* for him, oh merciful gods above—

Kesst shivered all over as he shoved up behind Eft, brought himself close. And then began stroking up his own swollen cock, with far more intent and speed than before. Bringing up as much thick seed as he possibly could, and gasping at the sight of it dangling down into Eft's opened crease, pooling there like it belonged. Like Kesst could truly, actually do this, pump himself out onto this, inside this...

And getting the seed inside would help, Kesst knew, in

making it easy and smooth—but even so, he jolted all over, and then very nearly blew, at the first touch of his slick head to Eft's waiting, quivering heat. Feeling it kiss and clench back against him, watching it suck his oozing seed inside, *his*, oh gods destroy him now.

"Good, Eft," Kesst somehow breathed, as he pressed just a little closer, watched his own glossy swollen head pumping out more, pulsing it into that tight spasming heat. "Want you nice and wet for me. Want you—*ack!*"

Because Eft had abruptly eased backwards onto Kesst, swallowing his entire head inside—and Kesst keened and moaned as he felt it, as his cock instantly flared, and flooded out more. Knowing where it was now, knowing its goal, and oh, Kesst could scarcely hold himself still, wanted to plunge himself deep, to feel even more of Eft around him, encasing him, consuming him whole...

"More," Eft growled, and Kesst audibly gulped as he stared, drank up the sight of it, of his own fat, familiar, pretty cock jutted just inside Eft's arse... and then sinking deeper. Sinking into dark slippery ecstasy, breath by breath, because Eft was pushing back, Eft was taking him, Eft was doing this, holy mother of all the clans and the earth and—

"Fuck," Kesst gasped, as he watched himself sink deeper, watched Eft swallowing him, impaling himself upon him. Deeper, deeper, oh this wasn't happening, this couldn't possibly be happening, it was hot, tight, teasing flesh all around him, clasping and caressing him, further and further, until...

Kesst bucked and howled at the feel of his bollocks touching skin, at Eft sinking him home, locking them together. And there was no more of Kesst to see, there was just Eft's gorgeous arse pressed flush to his hips, swallowing him whole. And flooding him with the most impossible sensation, with the most unthinkable heat and pressure, and with—

The rush of magic felt like a blow, like an uncontrollable

thunder unmaking Kesst, demolishing him. Encircling him in that sparkling golden warmth, together with this slick surrounding heat, and it was too much, it was so much, Kesst was so close, so desperate, he was about to—

His release flooded out of him in sharp, shrieking torrents, surging out again and again and again. Pouring Eft full of his hot sweet rapture, gushing and spraying, all of it caught and drunk deep into that impossible unthinkable clutch. Eft was drinking him, Eft was already scenting of him, Eft was jerking his own cock with a quick frantic hand—and now he was shouting too, his back arching, his tight heat rhythmically convulsing against Kesst's still-spurting cock, dragging out more seed, more wild choking euphoria. Until Kesst was utterly, entirely empty, his prick squeezing out nothing, his body still sparking all over with blazing, furious bliss.

And finally, somehow, it was over. Over, with Eft exhaling hard, his body sagging heavily onto the bed. But his grip on Kesst had tightened, dragging him down too, and Kesst couldn't stop shuddering at the feel of himself still there, still *inside* Eft, while his scent kept deepening on Eft's skin, oh, gods above.

Kesst's face was somehow buried in Eft's neck, his breaths inhaling, his teeth instinctively scraping against that sweet, sweaty skin. Wanting to taste more, needing more, more, *more*—and that was Eft's hand, spreading wide against the back of his head. "Do it," he whispered. "Please."

It was too much, too intense to bear, and Kesst dragged in one last, unsteady breath—and then sank his teeth deep. Breaking Eft's skin, and finding that glorious scent beneath, made shockingly real upon his tongue. He was in Eft, he could taste himself inside Eft, his own distinctive flavours already seeping into Eft's rich, succulent lifeblood. He'd become part of Eft, and now Eft would become part of him, and that would never change, never, ever...

Kesst couldn't have said how long he drank, gulping down that unthinkable liquid confirmation of this, of them, making it his own—but at some point it was strong enough, and he was sated enough, that he regretfully eased himself out of Eft's slack, flooded-wet arse, and drew his teeth from his neck. Instinctively licking and caressing the wound he'd made, until he could no longer taste freshness upon it, until he somehow knew it was sealed, with his own scent forever buried inside.

And without thinking, without hesitating, he grasped for Eft's pliant body, and turned him onto his back on the bed. Settling himself close on top again, flicking his hair out of the way—and then guiding Eft's mouth up to his own arched, bared throat. His own offering.

Eft instantly obliged, his teeth sinking strong and deep into Kesst's skin, his mouth hissing a low, garbled groan. And Kesst knew, with inexplicable certainty, that Eft would be tasting both of them in his blood now, would feel how the scent had deepened, gone fuller and richer than it had yet. How this, with their mutually exchanged seed and blood, freely blended and then drunk back in again, would be the strongest scent-sharing possible amidst their kind, beyond a total scent-bond. How now their scents would never, ever fade from one another, and would always be stronger than all the rest.

So Kesst revelled and gasped in Eft's low moans, the steady swelling of his own previously slackened cock. And when Eft finally drew away from Kesst's neck—dispensing with the licking, in favour of just healing the bite with his kiss—he looked just as stunned and overwhelmed as Kesst felt, his face and ears flushed deep, his lips swollen and stained with red.

"Fuck," he breathed, his voice hoarse with wonder. "What that did to our scents, Kesst. To yours. I mean"—he hauled in a breath—"I've already drunk your seed, so I didn't realize this would make so much of a—well. Forgot to mention that, did you?"

Kesst huffed a trembly laugh as he nipped at Eft's mouth, shook his head. "I didn't want you to think," he managed, "you had to let me do that, or—"

But Eft instantly nipped him back, bumping their foreheads together. "Ridiculous," he breathed. "You made it so good, Kesst. So damn good. You felt *incredible*."

Kesst felt Eft shiver all over as he spoke, as if in confirmation of those impossible, unthinkable words—and Kesst shivered too, a high-pitched noise escaping his throat. "Really?" he gulped. "You're sure? I mean, I barely even did anything, it was probably still completely rubbish for you, I should have—"

But that was another nip against his lip, sharp and decisive. "It was perfect," Eft whispered. "Thank you, Kesst."

Kesst shivered again, harder this time, his sheer disbelief now swirling, shaking his head. "You're sure," he croaked. "You're—"

"I'm sure," Eft cut in, his voice impossibly steady, as he pressed a firm, purposeful kiss to Kesst's mouth. "And if I—if we keep going, both ways... will it keep making our scents stronger, like this?"

His voice had gone a little uncertain again, shy, almost *hopeful*—and Kesst betrayed another full-body shiver as he nodded. "Of course it will, love," he murmured, as his affection—and relief—seemed to surge into his belly, his heart. "Deeper and deeper with every fresh bite and load between us. If you—if you really think you'd want it again?"

His own voice sounded shy, too, as if he were the blushing innocent once again—but then there was only bright, blistering awe as Eft nodded. "Oh, I want it," he murmured back, inhaling deep against Kesst's neck, while more hunger studded into his scent. "Maybe we could—take turns?"

Take *turns*. Good gods, Eft wanted to take turns. With that. With *him*.

And Kesst was suddenly, desperately clutching Eft close, and kissing him. His eyes prickling, his fingers stroking and dragging at Eft's back, his hair, his face—and then, before could stop himself, he spun around onto his hands and knees, and blatantly presented his own arse toward Eft. Not caring how brazen or greedy it was, because oh, oh gods, this was exactly what he needed. He needed that already-familiar, magnificent pole swiftly, eagerly finding him, settling its head close against his own frantically gripping heat, where it owned him, where it belonged...

And as Eft gently pressed forward, easing that slick head just inside, Kesst was somehow struck with a strange, stilted clarity, amidst the sweeping dizzying pleasure. Kesst had fucked Eft. His *mate*. And they were going to do it again? And again, and *again*?

"Oh, Eft," he moaned, as he smoothly, slowly slid backwards, impaling himself just the way Eft had, sucking that pole further and further, until it was buried balls-deep in his tight, hungry arse. "Oh, that feels so good. Love it filling me like this. Need it to pump me full of your seed. Need to be *flooded* with you."

Eft gave a hoarse, guttural groan, and then eased his full length back out, bit by bit, until he was just giving Kesst the head, taunting him with that exquisite teasing tension—and then he gradually slid his way back in again, while Kesst shuddered and squealed upon him. Glorying in the impossible sensation of being sweetly, purposefully pierced, skewered, jammed full to his utter limits... and screeching and flailing as a flying flare of magic shot him beyond, into the bright blinding abyss.

Behind him Eft was actually chuckling, the beautiful bastard, the sound warm, indulgent, affectionate. And already he was picking up speed, carving in faster and deeper, spearing Kesst whole with every long, perfect, powerful thrust.

Remaking him, remaking them, and Kesst would never stop adoring him for this, ever—

"Good gods," came a shocked, vaguely familiar voice from the door—and when Kesst shot a half-lidded glance over, he found a wide-eyed, open-mouthed Abjorn, standing together with Sigarr, another Ash-Kai, just outside the room. "Ach, how does this even *fit*?"

Abjorn was referring to Eft's monster cock, of course, which hadn't hesitated its smooth, unrelenting conquering of Kesst's arsehole in the slightest. And Kesst tossed his head as he arched his back and moaned, showing them just what this looked like, while also flashing a rather smug-feeling smile toward the door.

"Jealous, Abjorn?" he drawled, his voice hitching as Eft sank home again, making him shudder and quake. "You only *wish* you had a giant Ash-Kai cock splitting open your uptight Ka-esh arse right now, hmmm?"

He was immensely gratified by the instant flush on Abjorn's cheeks, and his furtive glance toward Sigarr beside him. And it distantly occurred to Kesst that there was undeniable interest in that glance, and also—wait—Abjorn *did* faintly scent of Sigarr, didn't he? But had Kesst ever seen them together before? Or seen Sigarr's fully hard cock? Perhaps not?

"Why don't you take pity on him, Sig?" Kesst blithely continued, between gasps, as he moaned and preened upon Eft's unrelenting onslaught. "I mean, there's no chance in hell your prick is as perfect as Eft's, but I am sure as hell not sharing him, and Abjorn obviously needs a good strong dicking-down. Maybe a few hard yanks on his chain, too."

And now it was Sigarr's face flushing, as he glanced uncertainly at Abjorn beside him. And then he jerked and lurched away, while Abjorn shot Kesst a look of purest loathing, and then rushed away after Sigarr down the corridor.

"You ridiculous hellion," Eft grunted behind Kesst, with

unmistakable amusement in his voice, as he drove in faster, his heavy bollocks slapping Kesst's skin, every thrust rearranging Kesst's insides with spectacular precision. "You *enjoyed* that, didn't you?"

Kesst moaned and gave Eft a few hard squeezes, arching his back a little more, sucking him deeper. "Fuck, yes," he gasped smugly, between thrusts. "All these bastards are going to be so damned jealous of me, they won't be able to see straight. And they don't even know the half of it, because—*ack!*"

That was once again a flare of Eft's magic, flooding through that plunging cock with stunning strength, and Kesst shamelessly shrieked and shouted and begged as Eft rammed in faster and harder. Giving him everything he wanted, everything he'd ever needed, oh gods please please please—

And then Eft skittered to a halt, his bollocks grinding tight, his voice rasping a guttural bark—and then he spewed out deep inside. Flooding Kesst with even more of his perfection, filling up his very innards with his fresh scent and his seed, marking him, swamping him, consuming him with sweet succulent safety.

And when Eft's hot mouth again found Kesst's neck, sinking his sharp teeth deep with one hard, purposeful bite, Kesst flailed and moaned, and then slowly sank into soft, shivering whirls of ecstasy. Gods, it was good, he had never felt so good in his life, so satisfied, so *whole*.

"You don't mind, do you, love?" he asked Eft, a little shyly, once Eft had finally drawn away from his neck, in favour of inhaling slow and deep against it. "If I gloat about you a bit? Show them what they can't have?"

He'd thought Eft had perhaps liked it at the time, though now he couldn't quite say why—but that was surely more hunger, swirling through Eft's scent. "I don't mind," he murmured, husky. "I—I like it. As long as it's still just m—"

Kesst could almost taste the wince in his magic, the way he

was biting off the word. And in return, he swiftly eased off Eft's length, hissing through his teeth at the feel of it, before twisting around to look at him, and taking his face in his hands. "It will always be just you, Eft," he said, slow and purposeful, holding his hazy eyes. "Always."

And that relief in Eft's magic, that quiet steady wonder, was all Kesst needed, everything he needed. "Good," he murmured back. "Gods, Kesst, I love you. My beautiful, generous mate. *Ég elska þig.*"

Kesst could only shiver, and nod, and swallow over the thickening lump in his throat. "Love you too, Eft," he croaked, as that prickling returned behind his eyes, and somehow escaped down his cheeks. "So much."

But Eft was wiping the wetness away, and gathering Kesst into his powerful chest, drawing him safe and close. "Good," he said again, as his hands spread wider against Kesst's back, stroking their familiar warm magic into his skin. "Now, as much as I hate to say this, we can't keep the sleep away forever, all right? Rest for me?"

Rest for him. And it distantly occurred to Kesst that he was definitely tired, and probably overwhelmed, and likely still in shock from quite possibly the most intense pleasure of his life. And that this was just what he needed, as always, Eft's strong arms around him, his warm stubborn safety inside him. Always.

"Anything you want, Eft," Kesst whispered, as he snuggled closer, and drifted away. "Anything."

THANKS FOR READING
AND GET A FREE BONUS STORY!

Thank you so much for joining me for Kesst's tale! Writing this book ended up being surprisingly cathartic for me, and it was just so rewarding to witness Kesst finally experiencing all the love, support, and validation he deserved.

I've been asked a few times about this, so I just thought I'd mention it here too—I am in full agreement with Eft that Kesst WAS a victim, even if Kesst sometimes felt ambiguous or conflicted about it himself (and was definitely not always a "perfect victim"). That conflict has been a huge part of my own experiences, so I did intentionally try to convey that—at least, until Eft comes along and starts to shift Kesst's perspective. Unconditional support like Eft's is so crucial to those in recovery, and I fervently hope that we as a culture can move more toward treating victims (including imperfect ones) with patience, empathy, and kindness.

I also did want to mention that this is just the start of Kesst's journey, and we see him often throughout my Orc Sworn series, especially *The Maid and the Orcs*. And in my next Orc Sworn book, Kesst's belligerent blood-brother Rathgarr will finally return to Orc Mountain (together with a brand-new "mate")... and of course, Kesst will have a LOT to say about that! I'm really looking forward to bringing these two brothers back together again, and solving some of the mysteries of their past.

Finally, if you're not quite ready to leave Orc Mountain yet, please come join my mailing list at www.finleyfenn.com for some fun extra content, including artwork from this book, and a free Orc Sworn story. I'd love to stay in touch with you!

FREE STORY: OFFERED BY THE ORC

The monster needs a sacrifice. And she's on the altar...

When Stella wanders the forest alone one fateful night, she only seeks peace, relief, escape. A few stolen moments on a secret, ancient altar, at one with the moon above.

Until she's accosted by a hulking, hideous, bloodthirsty *orc*. An orc who demands a sacrifice—not by his sword, but by Stella's complete surrender. To his claws, his sharp teeth, his huge muscled body. His every humiliating, thrilling command...

But Stella would never offer herself up to be used and sacrificed by a monster—would she? Even if her surrender just might grant her the moon's favour—and open her heart to a whole new fate?

FREE download now!
www.finleyfenn.com

ACKNOWLEDGMENTS

As always, I'm just so, SO grateful for my completely awe-inspiring community of readers, supporters, and friends. Getting to share our love of sexy orcs, books, and artwork together has been an unreal, unthinkable gift, and I am so thankful to every one of you!

I especially want to recognize the generous group of advance readers, proofreaders, and reviewers who've supported this book: Cookie, Erin, Jennifer N., Jen R., Judi S., Lauren Maunchley, Lexi K. Jordan, Serena, Sue Philips from Australia, and my all-time OG reader/cheerleader Amy F. And huge thanks to Rowan Phillips for providing his helpful contextual guidance, and to Þórey H. for her ongoing expertise with my Aelakesh (aka Icelandic)!

Of course, I must again mention Goddess Ruby Dixon, who has continued to give me appalling amounts of her time, insight, and support—thank you, Ruby! I'm also ridiculously grateful to the utterly brilliant Eris Adderly/Octavia Hyde, who I've finally wrangled into editing for me... life goal accomplished! (And if you haven't yet delved into Ruby and Eris' brilliant books, I cannot recommend them highly enough!)

I also want to particularly mention just a few of the many folks who've gone above and beyond to support me and my writing. A massive thank-you to MK, my second brain and voice of reason; Elizabeth, for all the delicious art and Discord support; Amy for being our much-needed Discord librarian; Katie for all the enthusiasm and entertainment (go follow her at Romantically Inclined, she's such a delight!); Coco and

Morning Dove for bringing all our orcs to life; and my many fabulous fellow authors who have given me so much of their advice and inspiration.

And finally, as always, I want to thank my own stubborn, sexy mate, who so generously helped me escape my own darkest past, and has kept me swimming in safety and reassurance ever since. I am forever grateful, my love.

AELAKESH PRONUNCIATION GUIDE

Ég elska þig (I love you)
    yeg EL-ska thig

Fallegur (beautiful)
    FAHT-leg-ur

Stórglæsilegur (stunning, elegant, magnificent)
    STOAR-glys-hil-e-ghur

Borðaðu (to eat)
    BOR-tha-thu

Morgunmatur (breakfast)
    MOR-ghun-ma-thur

Leggstu niður og þegiðu (Lie down and shut up)
    LHEGG-hstu NEE-thur ogh THEY-hi-thu

ALSO BY FINLEY FENN

THE LADY AND THE ORC

He's the most feared monster in the realm. And she's what he needs to win his war...

In a world of warring orcs and men, Lady Norr is condemned to a childless marriage, a cruel lord husband, and a life of genteel poverty—until the day her home is ransacked by a horde. And leading the charge is their hulking, deadly orc captain: the infamous Grimarr.

And Grimarr has a wicked plan for Lady Norr, and for ending this war once and for all. She's going to become his captive—and the perfect snare for Lord Norr.

There's no possible escape, and soon Lady Norr is dragged off toward Orc Mountain in the powerful arms of her greatest enemy. A ruthless, commanding warlord, with a velvet voice and mouthwatering scent, who awakens every forbidden hunger she never knew she had...

But Grimarr refuses to accept half measures—in war, or in pleasure. And before he'll conquer Lady Norr's deepest, darkest desires, she needs to surrender *everything*.

Her allegiance.

Her wedding-ring.

Her future...

And with her husband's forces giving chase, Lady Norr can't afford to play such a dangerous game—or can she? **Even if this deadly orc's plans might be the only way to save them all?**

ALSO BY FINLEY FENN

THE MIDWIFE AND THE ORC

Orc Mountain needs a midwife. And this devious, deadly orc is determined to find one...

In a world of recently warring orcs and men, Gwyn Garrett is a lord's daughter on a mission—to escape her lord father, dump her cheating betrothed, and pursue her true calling as a plant-obsessed midwife.

Until the night her brand-new house is invaded by an *orc*. A tall, taunting, treacherous monster, with sharp teeth, vicious claws, and gleaming black eyes. And worst of all, a blatant, brutal mission of his own...

He's come to court her.

Claim her.

Compromise her.

But Gwyn is far too clever to fall for this sneaky orc's schemes—right? Even if he moves like a graceful god, if his voice is sweet syrup in her ears. If his low, mocking laugh sparks something hot and reckless, deep in her soul...

It's hunger, it's *home*, it's everything Gwyn never knew she needed—but in its wake, there's only devastation. Defeat. And the realization that she's forever linked with this horrible orc, and his horrible plans...

And with the war. The fates of hundreds of women like her. And the truth that **Orc Mountain desperately needs her, and maybe this proud, lonely orc does too...**

ALSO BY FINLEY FENN

THE MAID AND THE ORCS

She's fallen for an angel... but he's mated to a monster.

In a realm of orcs and powerful men, housemaid Alma Andersson is drowning—in grief, debt, and drudgery. And when her awful employer makes his darkest demand yet, she flees for the forest, and tumbles toward her doom...

Until she's snatched to safety by a **huge, vicious green beast.**

An *orc.*

He's utterly terrifying, with his towering bulk, sharp teeth, and deadly black claws—but his touch is gentle, and his eyes are kind. And his scent is a deep, decadent sweetness, sparking a furious flame between them...

But it's only more disaster, because **Alma's shy, soft-hearted rescuer is already mated... to another** *orc.* A tall, silent, snarling monster named Drafli, who loathes Alma on sight, and clearly longs for her death.

Yet Drafli will do anything for his sweet mate, even if it means tolerating a weak, worthless human. So he makes Alma a cold, calculated offer: **he'll share his mate with her... but only on his terms.**

He wants her silence.

Her surrender.

Her servitude.

And with Alma's fate firmly in Drafli's ruthless hands, how can she face her own dark desires—or all the secrets hidden behind Orc Mountain's walls? **Can a lost, lonely housemaid come between two orcs... without being crushed?**

ABOUT THE AUTHOR

Finley Fenn has been writing about people falling in love for as long as she can remember. She creates steamy fantasy romance tales with cranky-but-sexy men and monsters, loads of angst and drama, a dash of mystery and action, and wholehearted happily ever afters.

When she's not obsessing over her stories, Finley reads everything she can get her hands on, and drools over delicious orc artwork (find her latest faves on Facebook at Finley Fenn Readers' Den). She lives in Canada with her beloved family, including her very own grumpy, gorgeous orc husband.

To get free bonus content, character illustrations, and news about upcoming books, sign up at www.finleyfenn.com.